Pouter

Mountain

Shine

\\Kelly Davenport//

Yaupon Press

This book is dedicated to

Lara, Jaime, and Liam

Chapter 1

Lige Worley hadn't been down off the mountain in so long he no longer knew the day of the week proper. Could have been a Tuesday but it sure did feel more like a Monday. May be a Wednesday though. He lay on the ground staring up at the big, boiling ball in the sky. Bright and big as punch. Perspiration already soaked his shirt, front and back. And the white patch of his forehead—the part usually covered with his hat-brim—burned like bacon sizzling in a hot pan. Damned sure knew better than to fall asleep out here in the open but then he knew he wasn't sleeping out there in the open. More like passed out from the shine. He tried to lick his dry lips, but there was not even enough moisture in his mouth to get the better of a postage stamp much less wet his lips. He looked again at the sun, shining above him to straight up twelve o'clock and the earth moved sickeningly underneath his large

1

frame. Only thing for it was to sit straight up, fast-like and take it head-on like running through hell. And that's what he did. He sat bolt upright and let the world spin. Let it spin. He could handle it better when it was all atwirl anyway.

He fumbled around in the grass surrounding where he'd lain for God only knew how long in a drunken stupor. Where was it? He found his hat, that had been easy but where was what he really needed? Hair of the dog! That's what he looked for now. There it was! Thank the good Lord for the sun this time for its glittering all over the glass of that bottle. Lige grabbed up the bottle like it was an injured baby and unscrewed the cap with his right hand— the one that's missing two of its fingers. He gulped the clear liquid with greed. His hand trembled and some of the *white lightnin* escaped from the side of his mouth and down his whiskered chin.

"BBhhhhaaaahhhh!" he exhaled a long satisfied breath.

Nobody, not nobody, can make it like I do. Unc Rayburn could and he's the one that teached me to right before he blowed himself up. Good thing he showed me first or the recipe'd be in the ground with him—in his head. Right purdy funeral too, for a man anyway. Lige crawled on all fours for about twenty feet and realizing the spinning was gone he sat up on his knees first and then lifted the rest of his body off the ground. Everything looked a little strange from the standing perspective but only for a few moments. Only until he became adjusted to his current height. He made his way to his shelter. Really the shelter was made from a few items he'd round up from the landfill. He meant to build him a little cabin, and he would do that too. One of these days. Not today, that was for certain, but one day. Soon maybe. What he had now was a good place. He had two poles set in the ground at diagonals—he'd paced it off at thirteen feet but he'd used his own feet to do the pacing which meant the space was quite a bit bigger than thirteen feet—anyway those poles were from a child's swing-set. The other two poles set in the ground at opposite diagonals from the first were some two by fours he scavenged from an old dog house. These poles he'd had to nail together to make them tall as the metal poles but that worked out just fine in the long run. He was the only one to see them anyway and they suited him. Suited him just dandy.

The real hard part about this shelter was waiting to find the covering for it. He couldn't even remember the times he went down to the landfill looking for suitable material for the topper. Ten, twelve, maybe even fifteen. Yes, fifteen. That number sounded right to him now when he thought about it. And then, eureka! There it was. A broken down trampoline. He recalled now how he'd laughed that day, beating his hat against his leg and hopping up and down like a little youngun on Christmas morning. Just what he needed and there it was. God provides for believers. Yes He does. Now, his stomach growled with hunger but he knew there was no need to try and eat anything heavy after last night. Had it only been one night he'd been out there laying flat out full and hydrated like a big-fat bellied starfish in the night and waking the next day skinny and dried out in the sweltering hot sun? Lige didn't truck to losing all these days. He had a calendar and he used to mark off the days with a carpenter's pencil but then he realized that he couldn't even be certain he'd marked off the right number of days.

He couldn't be trusted, could he? Something was wrong, real wrong, when a man couldn't even trust himself.

Grits. He could eat some grits. They'd probably do real good on his queasy gut. He made his way over to the live oak where he kept his food, his pantry. He'd driven ten-penny nails into the trunk of the tree and through the labels of the dry goods he kept way up in the top-most branches. Lige unraveled the twine that was attached to a jump rope that was attached to a piece of clothesline and let the bag of grits down until it was close enough for him to reach, opened the plastic zip-lock bag, scooped out an overflowing cupful of the meal, and then pulled on the twine until the bag was back in the upper part of the tree. It was safe there. Safe from bears. Now the coons were a little more trouble. He had yet to figure out a way to keep them away except to leave some scraps for them way off, away from his camp. They were a little bit lazier and a whole lot easier to console than the bears. He also had flour, sugar, coffee, fatback, pinto beans, butterbeans, lard and a few other food-stuffs and medical supplies up in the tree. And there was one other item. The piece that he hardly dared to call by name. A thing of beauty. And just thinking of it now made his mouth water. He was aware of the saliva rushing from all corners and crevices of his mouth. The mouth that only moments ago had been dry as autumn leaves. A country ham. His thought had been all along to save the ham for Christmas dinner but he knew that living alone as he did didn't require festivities. He could have Christmas dinner any day he decided to have it. Who was there to tell him no? No one, that's who. Ever since Eller died there'd been no one. Eller and the little baby both. Here one minute, gone the next. One thing he'd always wondered since they died. Did Eller kill the

4

baby or did the baby kill Eller? *Had to be one way or the other. Sure and certain they both died but who started the dyin? Eller was fine. The baby was fine. Then both of em was dead. Now, them funerals weren't purdy. No Siree.*

Lige pushed the thoughts of Eller and the baby out of his head. Well, not really out of it because they were never, in truth, out of his head, but to the back. He pushed them to the back. He would think about them later. He pulled the bladder off the hook where he hung it every night after filling it at the creek. The bladder was another wondrous find from the landfill. Before he found it, he had to keep his water in large tin cans and every morning there were all grades of insect life floating on the surface of the water and he could never tell what varmints had come to quench their thirst during the night. He needed to make another trip down there soon. See what he could come across. The day he found the bladder—well, he called it a bladder, he reckoned it was actually an enema bag, Eller used to call the one they had a hot water bottle and on cold nights, the kind that cut right through the walls, a body's skin and on down to the bone, she would fill it full of boiling water, wrap it in a dish towel and put it at their feet between them in the bed where they slept—he also found a tin cup and a dinner plate. There was nothing even wrong with them either. Except for one chipped place on the plate. Who throws stuff like that away? That was a real good day. Anyway, he needed to go down there again and see what he could find.

He poured some water into his cook pot and took it over to his little fire-pit. He moved the metal rack he'd taken off a beat up, bashed in grill, picked up his fire-stick and moved the ashes and cinders around and to the side, out of his way, and then added tiny pieces of kindling until

5

the tiniest fire caught and took. Slowly, a piece at a time, he added larger and larger pieces of wood to the fire until it produced a good, hot flame. He replaced the rack and set the cook-pot on top to wait for the water to boil. *I'm one rich sum-bitch! But what kind a sum-bitch gets the grits out a the pantry and leaves the coffee? A stupid, rich sum-bitch like him, that's who!* Lige stood up, knees creaking, hip screaming and made his way back to the live-oak for the coffee. He laughed at himself. Better to laugh than to cry. *A stupid, rich, and old sum-bitch, I reckon!* He knew he also needed to buy more supplies but before he could do that he was going to have to sell off the rest of this shine. Now that was another thing to add to his to-do list, which was getting longer by the minute. But if he could sell what he had left then he could buy three months' worth of supplies and enough to make another couple batches of the good stuff. Peach brandy too. The peaches were going to be plentiful and fat this year. There'd been just enough rain. Rainfall had to be just right for the peaches to be so grand. And there wasn't anybody didn't love some good peach brandy. Even the women-folk bought it and would drink it too. Yessir, he had plenty to do. A gracious plenty. He brought the coffee back to the fire-pit, poured the grits into the pot, watched them swirl around in the vortex of the boiling water before he stirred them around with the take-up spoon he used both to cook and eat with and then reached for his enameled coffee pot. The coffee pot hadn't been found at the landfill though. He paid good money for it at the Goodwill in town. Good money, precious money. He shook the right amount of grounds into the pot. He didn't need to measure. Eller always measured but he could do it by sight. By sight and feel. He knew when it looked and felt right. The right sleight of hand. In what seemed like an eternity to his stomach and a split second to his mind, his breakfast of grits and coffee was done. He took both pots with him to the shelter, leaving the fire to burn and sat on a lawn chair in the corner. The lawn chair was the old-timey kind with the green and pink and white strips of nylon going from one side to the other and then woven up and under with identical strips going from front to back. If you turned the chair upside down, and he had, you could see the metal fasteners stamped through the nylon and the metal holding it all in place. A person could get rich with ideas like that one. Simple and handy. That's what it took to get rich these days. Any days really. A thing had to be simple to make and handy to use. Nothing more, nothing less.

Lige had come up with some ideas like that over the years. Simple and handy inventions but every time he got excited about one of his ideas, something he meant to invent, somebody had beat him to it. *Every damn time! Every idea I ever had somebody beat me to it. Good ones too! Eller always said it meant I was smart. Just cause they beat me didn't mean I didn't think it first. I just needed to be faster next time. Not to keep it in my noggin so long before I made the invention. There she is again. Third time she's popped up today. I miss her. I wish I told her more what she meant to me. How much she meant. I don't reckon I ever told her. Not really. Did I show her? Did she know what she meant? Sometimes I get so mad and mean about that little baby. Whether it killed Eller or Eller killed it don't matter much—if it weren't for that little baby I reckon Eller would still be here.* Lige knew if he was going to get through this day, whatever the day was, he was going to have to stop thinking about the two of them. Thinking of those two didn't leave him in too good a shape no way he looked at it. If he didn't stop it and stop it right now, then he was going to end up sprawled out back on the ground again and he had too much to do. He couldn't risk it. It's a Wednesday. That's it. It's a Wednesday and it's going to be a Wednesday all day long. Wednesday's are friendly days. Middle of the road. That's the kind of day he needs a friendly, easy day. He opened the drawer of the nightstand he'd carried on his back all the way from the landfill sometime last year. The surface of the nightstand held the coffee pot, his coffee cup and his pot of grits but the drawer held the calendar. He leaned down close to peer into the drawer. The drawer was deep and the calendar was not on top like he'd thought it would be. He breathed in the drawer's essence and the smell was familiar. He smelled the smell with his nose, but he smelled it other ways too. He sniffed with his brain, inhaled with his stomach, breathed in with his mouth and slowly, tenuously was able to define the odor. He almost had it and then it whiffed away, dancing around in his mind like a forgotten broken legged ballerina in a music box. And then it wafted back to him. The tang of a wet burnt potato chip. Not the thin chips but the hearty, ridged ones. He felt the smack of the scent at the back of his throat and only after he felt it there did he taste it. The bouquet was at once repugnant and cloying. Sick-sweet, nauseating. But he could not refrain from taking it all the way inside himself. Where had he smelled this particular odor before? He knew he'd smelled the odor in Papa Worley's bedroom but he didn't know where or how.

He didn't know, couldn't place it. And then as his trembling hand reached for the calendar, the tears came. They came from the depth of some place way down inside of him that knew no words. Tongue-less, chord-less, speechless. This place could only feel. The place of sense, experience, awareness. Lige fell to the earthen-floor, turning the lawn chair as he smashed onto the surface of the small piece of the world that he believed he owned when in truth he owned none of it. Unless possession really did constitute ownership, if it did, then he owned this entire mountain. But he did not think of this right now, not in a real sense of the word because he could not think. He could only experience. For example, he felt the vibration come up, up and up from the belly of the earth and rumble through his very body. The vibration began the same way most things did, he supposed, easy and sneaky, making its way up and through until it became a tremor pulsing from his viscera and moving in straight lines from his torso to his shoulders and out to his fingertips and from the same core to his hipbones and out to his the ends of his toes. But the vibration stopped there, not leaving his body to return to the earth. Instead, the vibration stayed inside him, as he lay prostrate, moving from his abdomen to terminal points and back again to his abdomen to travel the same course until finally it coiled itself into a tight ball and rested in his groin. And there it stayed and he hoped it would stay for he never wanted to experience such as this again. He stood shakily for the second time that day. Wednesday. Took out the calendar and rifled again through the drawer being careful, oh so careful not to breath in its magic, its hoo-doo, oh so careful not to awaken whatever he'd just awakened, let it sleep, let it rest, let it be, and he found the carpenter's pencil and circled the third Wednesday of the month of August. That was the date. Middle of the road.

Chapter 2

Lige made his way down Pouter Mountain taking the same route he always took. Walking downhill, traipsing the same paths, crossing the same creeks, wending through the same brambles, hopping across the same rocks, bending under the same branches, and across the same fields as he always did. And as he left the miles behind him, he touched the same trunks of the same trees, leapt from his feet at the same places to grasp the same branches closest to his highest height, and stopped to pick up rocks from the same marker and from the same piles and throw them in the same directions as he did every trip down Pouter that he'd ever made. For Lige couldn't find comfort in any kind of change from any place, part or area of his life or of the life around him. He wanted, needed, everything he touched and everything that touched him to hold within its depths a familiarity that securely fastened both him and it to the earth and its safety. He needed every object and item in his realm to reassure him, to console him and to soothe him. And not only superficial consolation and soothing but deep down in the roots of his soul. Lige needed to know that the environment through which he moved and which moved through him was kindred just as sure and certain as were his own kinfolk. The inhabitants of nature, its flora and fauna, at one with his very own purpose. Lige never stopped to wonder about his purpose. Lige never questioned his motives, his hopes, his dreams, his goals, and neither did he ask if he even had any of these qualities inherent, or even exherent, for that matter because to him to be alive meant that there was intrinsically a motion-forwardness for what use would there be in moving backward. He did not ask how he reached for anything above or beyond himself. He simply believed that he did.

As he ambled along, pulling the empty wagon behind him, he did think about the past but he firmly resolved to keep Eller away from his thoughts. After yesterday, and a restless night that came on its heels he believed that if Eller occupied his mind today there would be so little of him remaining to render what lay ahead impossible. Today would be a busy day, filled with errands and shopping. He was to go down Pouter, into Mabry's Crossing to buy supplies and to the landfill. Of course, the trip to the landfill would come first because he would have no idea what he needed exactly until after he rifled through the discarded items there. While he knew he must make good use of his time and to be careful not to forget anything he must accomplish, he did not have to hurry. He had left just before daybreak, after eating a breakfast of grits and fried fatback, and knew if he was steady during his errands even allowing for a lunch in town then he would be back in his camp before sundown.

He allowed his mind to wander as he walked along a dirt path he'd travelled many times in the past. He knew this pass through would take roughly twenty minutes of his time and relaxed not having to be alert for entryways or landmarks that may have changed in some form or another since his last journey down the mountain. He could just unwind and allow his mind to take over. To go where it pleased, except for that one place. He thought first of his grandmother, Careen. Beautiful Careen Worley. Careen had been the only person in his life he had loved with abandon. With her, he could be Lige. He could let himself go. He laughed when he wanted, he cried when he wanted, he screamed when he wanted. With Careen, he had never had to be careful. He never had to hide his thoughts or feelings. She accepted everything and expected nothing. And Careen took the whole world of troubles into and onto herself and never, ever did they affect her. She was unafraid, unabashed and unbridled. As was usual when Lige thought about his grandmother, he became split, divided, and multiplied all at once in his thinking. He never knew where the hub of his focus was. Where to begin? Lige took a deep breath, closed his eyes, not tight until the lids were black in front of them but loosely so that they were warm and red in the sunshine. He kept them closed, while walking slowly along, until Careen's face came up to the forefront of his mind and the vision of her danced in front of his forehead just between his physical eyes, to his metaphysical gaze and he saw her clearly. He saw her in detail but his mind examined her wholly at first and then took her to pieces. When he fixed his eyes on her whole face, he saw a raven-haired Indian priestess. That's the way he thought of her. He knew that she'd never, in fact, been a priestess but that fact did not change the image in his mind. Whenever he recalled her this way, her hair, long and lustrous, blew in the wind— straight out and around the left side of her face. In this depiction, her features appeared to have been carved into the flesh of a large acorn, or sculpted from cedar. Her sharp, angular brow and cheek bones making a pointed contrast against the softness of her large, limpid black eyes and full, supple bronze-rose lips. When he saw these same features in pieces, however, though he saw much the same characteristics, he saw images of eyes twinkling mischievously, lips somewhat thinned, pulled in laughter,

12

exposing large, white teeth. A pink tongue stuck out at him when he found her hiding spot during one of their games.

He had loved her implicitly and cherished the memories they'd made together but as most often happens with unreserved emotion truths are told, secrets are spoken and trust is absolute and unconditional. Careen never questioned whether Lige was too young to bear the brunt of such substance. She, to her way of thinking, knew that he belonged to her in a way that no other person on earth belonged to her. Not even Careen's daughter, Lige's mother, Caroline could come close to sharing the edge that Careen and Lige did. He was her Knight, her Bishop, her Rook, and though neither knew it at the time, he was also her King. All others were pawns. They were dispensable. Of course, Careen loved Caroline but the love she felt for her did not include or involve understanding. To be fair and truthful though, Caroline had never understood Careen and gave cause to wonder if her lack of understanding included love. Ah yes, there they came. The others. Lige had come to understand that he could never think of her without also thinking of them. Caroline and Papa Worley. And of all the secrets told to his young ears, with the expectation of his grasping the meaning, the true meaning, and to be able to process the information about the others without in turn actually turning it in and on himself, the ones that involved Caroline and Papa Worley were the most dangerous and self-damning to Lige. Careen couldn't have understood that or she would never have divulged them, would she have? Careen who wore ARMY boots, even under her fancy dresses. Careen who rode an Indian motorcycle at breakneck speeds and without a helmet. Careen who loved only one other person other than Lige.

Lige had been no more than eight years old when she took him up upon her lap, as much as was possible for he was a large boy even then, and whispered in his ear. *I don't love Papa Worley. He's not your real grandfather. I hate him. He hates me. Your mother is not a good person. Your mother is weak. I love Corporal Adams. He loves me. Your mother is sick too much. She will probably die soon. Your Papa Worley beat me once until my back looked like fresh, bloody ground beef. He beat me because he can't control me. Corporal Adams is your mother's father—your grandfather. He's dead and buried under a live oak somewhere in South Carolina. His wife found my letters to him and sent them back to me. She told me he had died of a fever. Told me never to send another letter. Your mother looks like him but she doesn't act like him. Papa Worley married me because I was already... .* Careen didn't say everything at once though; she fed him bits and pieces of back story until in many ways he'd constructed the plot himself, in an eight year old's mind and in an eight year old's way.

Lige crossed the last creek before he would come down into the valley—come out into Mabry's Crossing. He needed to rest a minute. Catch his breath and clear his mind. *Damn it all to hell! I'd a been better off to of thought about Eller instead of Careen. Why can't nothin just be good all the way? Everything's got to always be stained with something else. Damn it all!* He pulled his bottle from his back pocket, uncapped it and took a long drink from it. Why can't a body just turn off the mind? Just shut it down like a machine. It's got to always be thinking of something. What about all of us folks who don't have much good to dwell on and then what little good there is has always got to be mixed in with the other, the bad. He figured he might as well go on ahead and finish with the memory. Let it play itself out.

Careen was a person who didn't let things ride. She wouldn't be bested. She believed in an *eye for an eye; a tooth for a tooth.* She believed the parts of the scripture that suited her and the rest she didn't. Careen thought that she was the one who made the judgments. She didn't believe the part in the bible where God said to leave the wicked be, that soon you would look for them and they would be nowhere to be found. She didn't believe that part. She didn't believe it when God said V*engeance is Mine.* Or if she did believe those parts, then she believed that God was making those statements to others—not to Careen Worley. She was special. She was a member of the Cherokee Nation even after it was no longer called the Cherokee Nation. And vengeance was hers! Lige recalled how Papa Worley took Careen's Indian motorcycle into the barn and dismantled it piece by piece. He took her bike apart and ended up with so many bits and pieces and parts and wires and cables that no one would ever be able to put it back together again. Like Humpty Dumpty—all the king's horse and all the king's men couldn't put Careen's motorcycle together again. Lige recalled how Careen had stood at the kitchen sink staring through the glass panes in the window in front of her. What was that song she hummed as she stood there with her hands holding tightly to the edge of the enameled sink? Her hands held the sink so tightly that the points of her knuckles went white where the blood drained away from the bone. But the song—the song she hummed came from deep inside her body, the base of her body, and flowed out through her esophagus and up through her larynx, escaping her beautiful mouth and when the song, the melody met the air it became the most beautiful piece of music he had ever heard and he had never heard more or even as beautiful since. He reckoned he would never recall the piece but he could easily call up the tune. Almost without his realization, he began to hum the song now.

Lige cut off making the music as he stepped from the edge of the woods into the clearing just on the fringe of Mabry's Crossing. He stood for a few moments allowing his eyes to adjust to the brightness of the sun after being under the canopy of trees and overgrowth of the forest. Go ahead, Lige. Finish the recollecting. Finish it and let's get a move on. There's a gracious plenty to do; the whole day's stretching out there ahead. Lige closed his eyes and held tight to the wagon-handle. He felt his head whirl a bit but nothing in the way of yesterday's experience. After Papa Worley took Careen's bike apart, and after Careen stood there at the sink humming that hauntingly, amazingly beautiful tune, Lige believed everything was over between his grandparents. He assumed that Careen would have no recourse against Papa Worley. She made the grandest dinner that evening. Roasted pork, glazed carrots, and boiled red potatoes almost floating in fresh butter and flaked with parsley from the garden. For dessert there was lemon pie. Careen served the dinner, herself—a fact that didn't become apparent until the next day. In fact, no one thought anything of it until Papa Worley did not come down for breakfast, nor did he join them for lunch. Finally, Lige's mother said she would go and see about her father. As soon as Caroline stepped from the room, Careen looked at Lige with a raised eyebrow and a smile on her face. Momentarily, a scream was heard coming from Papa Worley's bedroom—a scream that made Lige's neck hair to stand on end.

Careen, stood calmly from the table, smoothed her skirt, and made her way upstairs. Lige followed closely behind her but stood in the hallway watching and listening.

"Mama! He's dead! Daddy's dead."

"Why yes, I reckon he is."

"That's all you can say? Your husband's layin there dead!"

Lige shook his head now; trying to rid it of the image it still held of what he'd seen when he peeked into that bedroom. Papa Worley sat in his armchair, with his pants half on, his shirt unbuttoned, his shoes and stockings off. He appeared to have been frozen in motion. But it was his tongue that Lige had never been able to purge from memory. The tongue, to equal degrees black and white— black near the back and white toward the front— protruded from his mouth. The upper part of the tongue so swollen that it resembled the underbelly of a fat toad sticking out and resting on the bulge of his chin. And Papa Worley's eyes were not even similar to the eyes Lige was accustomed to; they appeared to have a white membrane covering them so that the dark pupils were barely visible.

Lige stepped back under the covering of the tree-line, vomited and then took another large swig of shine. He wiped his mouth with the back of his hand and gulped down some more of the clear liquid. His stomach began to feel warm and comforted and he stepped back out into the warmth of the sunshine and when he looked up at the sun determined it was only a little before nine. May as well mosey on over to the landfill. He needed a horse and wagon but God knows he couldn't take care of an

animal—he could barely take care of himself and that's
the truth.

Chapter 3

The landfill was almost as common to him as his campsite up on Pouter and when he turned the last bend in the road before the dump opened up to him he instantly felt at ease. There'd be no one out here pilfering about; there never was. A couple times in the past, someone had come around to chuck some household item or another. Once, someone stopped by and hurled a sofa over the edge and Lige watched it as it turned end over end several full times before landing near the bottom of the heap. Lige waited for the truck to pull away and drive off out of sight before going over to inspect the piece of furniture. What he wouldn't have given to have been able to haul that lounger back up the mountain but he knew even on one of his good days it would be impossible. The piece was just too large, too heavy. He recalled now how he wiggled the arm pieces around and one of them moved loosely like a tooth ready to be spit out from between somebody's gums. He seriously considered taking the sofa apart and hauling it up Pouter in pieces. He knew it would take several trips though. Pouter wasn't the largest mountain in the area but she sure was steep and he wasn't getting any younger for sure. In the end, he'd done the only thing he could have done and that was to begrudgingly leave it behind. Another time, a young couple had come around to leave a headboard to a bed. That headboard had been in perfectly good shape too. Sometimes Lige pondered other people's logic but that kind of thinking didn't do him too well. Who was he to judge what they did, anyway? Most times he had a difficult enough time just keeping his own mind straight and sometimes, many times, he was sure he didn't succeed even in that.

Lige entered the area where he usually found the most where household items were concerned. The larger items like furniture, that is. He was disappointed. There was a chair with one leg missing. A coffee table, a piece of an old countertop and an ottoman. The ottoman might be a good find after all though. He didn't really have a decent armchair to use with it but who knew when one would show up out here. Better to have the ottoman ready for when one did appear. That was his logic. Be prepared. You just never knew when what you needed would come in out of nowhere. Just like falling from the clear, blue sky. He moved over to the right a little to see what might be on down the line. He saw something protruding the slightest bit out from under some kind of fabric. Drapes, maybe? The protrusion glinted in the bright sunshine as if the sun's beams had all twisted up together, making a tightly coiled, taut rope, and focused all its strength and power on that one object. That one object to the exclusion of all others. Nothing else in the landfill came to the fore with that piece glistening and twinkling at him as if it desired nothing more than for him to pick it up. To take it up from its spot of degradation. He fancied that the piece, whatever it was, actually had a thinking brain and a manner by which to communicate its thoughts directly to his own mind. Lige located a poking stick from the brushes and began prodding and nudging around the shimmering gleam. He quickly found that the shining part was connected somehow to a larger piece that was made of some heavy type of black metal. Iron? He moved the stick in such a way as to come up from underneath the metal portion of the thing and pulled upward. Lige was excited with the thrill of discovery. When the apparatus came loose from under the drapes and a couple inches of mud he clearly recognized it. *It* was one of those fancy ashtrays! The kind that rested in the tray of a tall pedestal. He immediately began to figure a way to fit it in the wagon without breaking it on the way back up Pouter. Of course, he knew the ashtray would hang off the edge of the wagon no matter which way he fitted it in, but he aimed to have it. One way or another. Another question was whether to clean it up in the creek over behind him or wait until he got back home. He would do it now. Maybe knock some of the weight off of it if he cleaned the mud clods away. He pulled the ashtray all the way out from under the pile, dragging the drapes part of the way out with it far enough from the rest of the garbage to make it possible to separate the two. He threw the drapes to the side and set the ashtray up in front of him just as he would if it were in his camp. Who would throw away such a beautiful piece of furniture? There was no accounting for some folk's taste, he was now more certain than ever. He turned the ashtray upside down just to make sure that he was right in his thinking that it couldn't be taken apart. He carried with him both flat and Phillips-head screwdrivers and a couple wrenches for things like this. The base would come off but the rest had to stay together and as he further examined it he decided it would be best to just leave it all in a piece.

He picked the metal part up in one hand and held the glass ashtray carefully in the other and walked down the gentle slope of the creek-bank to make his way to the water. The water was deep enough to immerse the structure completely and he held it under, slightly swishing it around to shake off as much of the mud as possible before having to scrub it away. The glass part cleaned up easily but the rest was more difficult because of the intricacy of the design. Lige had never seen anything as beautiful in his life—even in Careen's house—and as he brought it up for the final time from under the water, he believed that no other person had ever found such a rich item of décor. He was a fortunate man; a man of fortune. He laughed as he played with the word and turned to head back up the rise of the slight hill. What he then saw was such a sight of utter horror to him that the sheer force of it knocked him flat to the ground. He heard a woman's shrill bawling and he thought it came from the left but then as soon as he had the thought he believed it must be coming from the right. But what he looked up into made the importance of the screaming recede to last place. He was no longer holding either part of the ashtray and though he had no recollection of letting it go he knew its weight was in neither hand. The heft of the base no longer pressing against his leg. He was once more aware of the shrieking and wanted to tell the woman to shut the hell up. He had a real problem here on his hands and didn't need her making things worse. But then just at the moment he opened his mouth to say those things he realized that he was the one making the racket. He was the one crying like a howling female and he would have been embarrassed had he not known that in dealing with what he had before him he was in fact doing the best one could expect.

A woman lay naked in front of him. He had never seen a woman, any woman, with no clothes on, except Eller. And even then, Eller required a certain shade of darkness. This woman was completely naked, not a stitch of clothing anywhere on or around her, in broad daylight laying on a creek-bank. But that wasn't the part that made his guts unravel. He glanced quickly around, checking his environment. Was he alone? *God, please let me be by myself. No, wait, I take that back. Please don't let me be by myself. I can't handle it. Not none of it! Amen.* But he was alone. Lige's legs trembled and he knew they wouldn't hold him if he tried to stand so he crawled on all fours toward the woman. When he came up even with her he took in everything about the scene at once and then took it to pieces the way he always thought about things. The whole thing and then the pieces, the bits. He saw her eyes open and fixed on the blue sky above her but even that was not a good sign for he also saw the gnats were already inside the eyes. Already eating away at the soft, spongy balls. He saw that her eyes were blue. And dead. She was a black-haired girl. Black hair and blue eyes, that uncommon combination that was always striking even on a plain woman but this woman had been a thing of beauty. He could tell that she had been even as he looked upon her corpse. And still, he was ashamed by her nakedness. He shouldn't be looking at her. She should be covered up. She shouldn't be here like this. His eyes traveled downward from her face and rested on her throat. He didn't want to look further down—down where her breasts would be. He stared at the neck and saw the bluing of fingerprints all along the length of it. Someone had choked her and there was a purple mark on her jaw and the jawbone itself was crooked, unhinged. Murder. She'd been murdered and left at the dump. *Sweet Jesus! Somebody done killed this girl. What do I do? Need to leave. Fast.* Lige stood on shaky legs, looked back toward the ashtray, and filled with indecision felt a tear streak its way down his leathery face. *Stop cryin boy!* He started for the ashtray. He would gather up his belongings and head on out, head on back up the mountain. He'd come back another day for supplies. He didn't recall anybody seeing

23

him come in so all he had to do was make his way back out unseen and there'd be nothing to worry about. Somebody else could happen up on this girl and that somebody else could deal with it all. Not him. He didn't have what it took to handle something like this. He'd had enough grisly mayhaps to last a lifetime, more than a lifetime. He wasn't aiming to add this one to that pile of troubles. No siree!

He turned his back to the dead girl and retrieved his ashtray. Just before he turned back to make his way up the incline, he paced a few steps away from the spot where he stood. He'd go up the hill a little farther down. Maybe that way he wouldn't have to look at her again. He knew she couldn't see him but he felt as if her dull, lifeless eyes pierced straight into the quick of his soul. And they, to him, were full of reproach, recrimination and even blame. *Damn it all to hell! I ain't done a sumbitchin thing here! I just come to get me some stuff for my place! And here you are big as punch and deader than four o'clock! Damn it all!* He took a couple more steps away from the grassy knoll where she lay. He still saw her image behind his eyelids. Had all that thinking of Careen and Papa Worley made this happen? Was it all some kind of portent, an omen. He should've known not to spend all that time thinking on them because every time he did think about all of that from the past some hideous happening came up out of nowhere. One time he'd gotten the mumps and one of them dropped into his ball sac. Horrendous pain, that was. Another time, that old lady down the street died in the garden. And then there was that one time, the time when Clayton got choked on that chicken bone and afterward when he regained his breath went out to the hen-house and stabbed every laying hen he could get his hands on. Careen had beat Clayton with the fire poker until she almost killed him. Aunt Case had to pull her off and there'd been blood streaming from a nasty cut on the top of his forehead. Lige recalled how when Clayton had laughed afterward his teeth were stained with blood. And now this time, he came up on a naked, dead girl.

He began to make his way up the hill and heard the mew of a baby lamb. Lige was lightheaded and faint from the recent events and discovery. He pulled out his bottle, thinking that he should have taken a few swallows before now and if his wits had been about him to where he was any account to himself he would have. He tossed back three large swigs and almost immediately felt a little easier in his mind. A bit more settled. Everything seemed clearer and brighter. The world was a mite happier place. And then he heard the lamb again. *What in the Devil's God-Awful hell was a lamb doin back in here?* Lige stopped and turned in the direction of the sound. And the worst part, other than hearing the noise to begin with, was that the lamb was on the other side of the dead girl. Of all the craziness he could have come up on today, he had to stumble upon a dead body and a crying lamb. He should've stayed up on Pouter. Still holding the ashtray, he screwed up the courage to walk back over to where the girl lay on the crest of the hill and even though his real mind knew there was no way that she could have moved, to his other mind, the one that was wont to tricks and superstition, she appeared to have stirred. Of course, that was impossible but his mind was fixed on its belief. Once again, he set the ashtray down making a full front-on approach straight toward her. There was no other way with a dead person. You just had to go straight up to it— face it. And for the first time, with modesty to the back of him, he noticed that the girl was twisted at the waist in such a way that her buttocks faced him, her belly faced the sun and her face faced the tall branches of a white pine. Now, standing directly above her, he found the source of the soft but persistent whimpering.

Lige was aware of the trembling that came over him, causing every piece and part of his body to violently quake. He was aware too of the bilious vomit that for the second time of the morning rose up through his throat and spewed from his mouth. And then he was unaware of what happened next because the next cognizant moment he had was of him laying sprawled out beside the dead girl, staring up through the white pine and into the clear sky. Apparently, he'd fainted and he imagined that he'd plunged to the ground like a tightly corseted woman, but even he knew that with his height and weight he could never manage such refinement of grace. He was never afterward certain whether the sight of the tiny, gray body of the infant or the spectacle of the exposed umbilical cord had caused him to faint. He took another extremely long swallow of the shine because he knew what he had to do next. He found the end of the cord that was attached to the child and dug around in his front pocket for his pocket-knife. Lige saw his fingers shaking violently before he reached into the other front pocket and removed a box of matches. The first match struck, the sulpher exploding onto the back of his hand before he lost the flame. He struck another and ran the small blaze along the knife blade, sterilizing it the best he could. Still his hand quivered. He took that hand, held it steady with his other, not much more stable hand, and he bent to the task before him. He pulled the cord to him and though he wanted more than anything not to look at the horrid thing, he couldn't help but gawk. It was much bigger around than he would have thought and the color, or colors more like, were just regular colors but the way they twisted around the piece of humanity made them appear grotesque. He needed to vomit again but there was nothing left in his stomach. The alcohol must have been immediately absorbed into his bloodstream. There was purple, blue, red, black and gray. *Lige just play-like it's a real long turkey neck. That's all it is. A turkey neck. A turkey neck. You can do it. Wait a minute here! What can I tie it off with? I got to tie it off.* He glanced again at the little baby's mama and crawled up and around to her head. He took the blade of the knife and whacked of a section of her hair. He tied a tight knot at each end of the lock and then went back to the baby. He picked up the fat umbilical cord and kinked it like a garden hose, and then sliced straight through it with his knife. He felt his throat constrict and his stomach heave. *No time for pussyin out now. Finish what you started boy!* Lige gripped the lock of hair in his large, callused hand and wound it tightly around the cord close to the baby's belly and then tied it off. Good. There. It was done. Later, when he tried to go back over the rest of that morning, he could only make educated guesses. He must have picked up the ashtray and the baby, climbed the hill with them both, put them in the wagon, unearthed the drapes, laid the baby and the ashtray on top, leaving a section to cover it all up with and made his way back up Pouter Mountain. Home. And he knew he had to have finished off the bottle of shine he'd carried down with him because when he'd reached his campsite and felt for the bottle it was empty.

Chapter 4

That first night, Lige sat on the ground under and at the front edge of his shelter holding the tiny infant who no longer even had enough strength to whimper. Before it had stopped whimpering though, he heard it making a strange noise. A noise he'd never heard before or since. Almost like the smallest creature in the universe trying to clear its throat. Ach-ach-ach-hach, ach-ach-ach-hach. And he heard it repeated until the voice was still, depleted, and silent. Was it hurt? Surely, to lie out in the open the way it had next to its dead mother for God only knew how long had been tragic on some level—maybe to its soul—maybe some other way. Who was Lige Worley to think of, much less speak on, another's soul? He couldn't even deal with his own soul. He was afraid of his soul and he was afraid of this newborn child's too. He didn't know which frightened him more. But at that moment, he had to concentrate on feeding this baby. What could he feed it? How could he feed it? He hadn't thought of any of that when he'd fled the scene. All he had thought of was to get the baby out of that place, to safety, up on Pouter. He'd picked her up, and then stooped to pick up one more thing, before grabbing the glass part of the ashtray and put it in the large back pocket of his overalls and the base of the ashtray in the other hand.

For the moment, he didn't think of the third article he'd carried up the mountain with him. It still rested against his right butt-cheek between the fabric of his overalls and his skin. He looked down into the baby's face and started to cry. Not a loud, raucous sobbing like earlier in the day, but a gentle, tender weeping. Had he saved this

child only to bring it home with him to starve? Again he
prayed to the God he trusted and believed in. The only
entity other than himself he'd ever had to trust. Well, at
least since Careen died it had only been him and God. But
then of course, that was not counting Eller. He trusted
Eller but they didn't talk much. Eller had been such a quiet
spirit of a woman and if the truth be told he wouldn't have
chosen her for a wife except there'd been nobody else
after Danceray. He was of age, she was of age and it just
fell to them to marry one another. And he knew, had
always known, Eller would never have even chosen him if
Rooster had not betrayed her so wickedly. Rooster and
Danceray had betrayed them both. As Lige's mind toyed
with an attempt to define the love the two of them
shared, his intuition teased out the answer and the guilt
he'd always felt for not loving her enough was lifted off his
shoulders and from his heart. But right now, he needed to
talk to her. Needed to ask her a few questions. More than
anything, he craved for her to touch his shoulder and tell
him the right way to do by this little youngun. *Eller, I ain't
got no experience with nothin like this. You know how I
am. What I am. But I don't want for this youngun to go
dyin like its mama did. Eller, you should a seen it. No, I take
it back. I don't never want you to have to look on nothin
like what I seen today. But I got to feed this here baby. Can
you go talk to God? Maybe ast him for me in case he ain't
hearin me? Just in case cause I ain't got much more time
to figure it all out. Oh, and I hope you and our little one's
doin good up there in heaven. I'll be seein you both one a
these days.* Lige opened his eyes and looked back down
into the baby's face. It was true; the baby didn't appear to
be in pain. He pushed on different places and it didn't cry
out. As he watched her face, he saw the miniature eyeballs
move in their sockets behind thin lids, and her petite

mouth pinched itself up and made small, sucking movements and sounds. Thank God it's still living.

Eller's voice, close to his ear—maybe inside his ear—spoke to him then. *"Take her to Salter Ridge. It's the onliest way," she said. "No! I can't be traipsing in over yonder. You know they don't want me." "Well, sit right where you be if'n you want her to die in your arms." "Why do you always have'ta be so cantankerous?" "Take her to Salter Ridge. Danceray can help." If'n I go on Salter, they a kill me dead." "And if'n you don't, that babe'll be dead by daybreak!"* Lige glanced down again at the innocent face. The baby hadn't done anybody any wrong. He couldn't let her die, could he? Then he'd have that sin on him too, along with all the rest. *"I'm sorry Eller. You ain't cantankerous. It's me what is. I'll go tonight."* He listened for her soft voice but it didn't come again. She was gone. Lige knew, however, that he had to do as she directed. Hadn't he asked her to talk with God? God must have told her what to tell him. Maybe he would come back down off the ridge, maybe he wouldn't; it was just a chance he would have to take.

He laid the baby down on the sleeping mat in front of him and stood to gather his things. What would he need to take with him? The first thing he grabbed was a fresh bottle of shine. He put it in the front of his overalls and started to walk away but then went back and took out two more bottles and a jar of peach brandy. He'd give the brandy to Danceray. The other two might appease Clayton and Tater long enough for him to make a clean track back down Salter Ridge toward Pouter. Either that or it'll rile them up enough to finish him off. How long had it been since he'd laid eyes on Clayton and Tater Shifflett anyway? Ten years? More like fifteen? Something like that anyway.

He didn't have time to cipher it out right now; he could think on it on his way down the mountain or up to the ridge. Lige felt a fast-running chill travel down his spine. Clayton was one he could handle if it was only the two of them in a fair fight but there was nobody he knew of who could undertake a fight with Tater and come out of it. Tater was one mean son of a bitch. And no fight with him was fair. Story had it that when Tater discovered Missy Ann, his first wife, squirreling away coppers and silver money, he took his hunting knife, cut her from stem to sternum, reached in, and snapped off a rib, saying, "I be needin that back now, bitch!" all before her heart stopped beating. Lige shuddered with cold fear, felt his entrails begin to vibrate. He stopped where he stood, constricting his anal sphincter against shitting himself. The last time he shat his pants was childhood and if there was any way he could keep from it now he aimed to. Lige knew that to control his bowels meant he needed to regain control of his thoughts, and began to think of Danceray. Danceray, beautiful, graceful, lithe, Danceray. She was everything her name suggested but even her name could not hold a candle to the person she was. Or the person she had been all those years ago. Lige's mouth went dry and he took the bottle from his front top pocket and unscrewed the cap. He realized that he'd drank enough of the shine that day to be drunk as Cooter Brown by this time but he was, astoundingly, still sober.

Danceray would have been his choice of a bride—
sorry Eller—if he could have had her, that is. They'd all played together as children. Clayton, Tater, Rooster, Danceray, Eller, Otis, Racine and Lige. Missy Ann and Fred Jr. had been a few years too young for them to include in their games. But Missy Ann hadn't been too young for

Tater to marry up with when it all shook out, had she? Rooster had got Danceray. But he couldn't think about Rooster just then either. Thinking about Rooster would make him lose his nerve where going up on Salter Ridge was concerned and then that little baby would surely die. He couldn't face another death. Much less another death that was his fault. Even Eller and the baby's death came right back to him. If he'd gone and got help right from the beginning they would still be alive. He'd have his wife and the child and maybe other children too. That baby had been his and Eller's first and last. A little baby boy. Lige closed his eyes, trying to conjure up an image of the baby, and came up with a shadowy likeness. He recalled that the boy had a great amount of silky, black hair on his head and he had dark eyes. Most babies had blue eyes at first, but not that one. He couldn't be sure about it at the time because one can never really tell about a baby that young but he entertained the notion that his son looked like Careen. Careen of the Cherokee Nation. Careen of the wild. Careen who wouldn't be, couldn't be, held back or held down. He knew there was a fever going around. They all knew about the fever. That old wider-lady over on Pinter Mountain had already died from it and two little school children down in Mabry's Crossing had too. But even when, after delivering the baby, Eller couldn't get out of the bed, and stayed there for far longer than was customary; even when she couldn't hold down food or drink, they'd both thought it was simply a part of the after-effects of childbirth. And then the baby—the little feller hadn't even been named—couldn't take to the breast. He should have listened to his gut instead of his mind and Eller's. He should have gone for help. But he hadn't listened to his gut; he hadn't gone for help and they both died. And the baby was buried in a grave with a marker bearing no name. He almost named him himself but that seemed to go against Eller some way for he had no way of knowing for sure what she would have wanted.

But this little baby here—the one that was still breathing—was the one he had to think about now. Eller was right. If he didn't go to Salter Ridge now, this minute, the baby would run out of time. Lige knew too that this was one chance, one opportunity, one hope, of finally doing something right and good. Maybe if he helped this little youngun, then God would be able to forgive him for the wrongs he'd done. And even if God didn't decide to forgive and forget, then he knew he might be able to start on forgiving himself. He wouldn't forget though—he couldn't ever allow those terrible deeds of atrocity to slip out of his mind to slither away into the sea of forgetfulness—because if he ever once did, he would risk sliding back into those old ways and he would rather die than to do that. Those deeds of wickedness, breathing the hot breaths of iniquitous indignation and the molten spittle of righteous anger and blame, had been what had chased him up onto Pouter Mountain in the first place and when he set up camp all those years ago he fancied he heard the demons as they sat around the shelter, hissing and laughing. They laughed at him and because of him but always, always they were just outside his reach. At first, Lige had attempted to chase the evil spirits of the fiends away running in all directions face first into the darkness where they belonged but his efforts had been futile for as soon as he could run one off another two replaced it. Over time, he had tamed the dark, demonic forces until they receded on their own, skulking away, gliding on the undersides of soft bellies into the brush and he imagined back to the core of the earth, back into the cavernous

33

womb of the earth's core, and to their homes in the land of hell's anguish. But every now and then, they returned and on those nights he built fires all around the shelter to surround and cover him in safety. They had been gone for months now but one never knew when they would come again; that was one of their strongest and most effective of weapons against him, and all of mankind, he reckoned.

He needed to stop thinking of such and make plans to head down the mountain. Most important, he had to figure out how to safely transport the baby from Pouter to Salter Ridge. He had carried her up the mountain atop the pile of drapes he'd put into the wagon at the last minute. He then covered the baby, hardly as big as a can of salt, with the edging of curtain material until they'd gone into the tree-line and started up the thin, dirt path and then he'd carried her close to his chest the rest of the way up to the campsite. But he knew that to take her up on Salter in the wagon would not be a good idea. What would a woman do? What would Eller do? He scanned the area in and around the shelter looking for, hoping for, an idea. His eye landed on the clothes pile between his sleeping mat and the night-chest. It just might work! He walked over and picked up a sleeveless tee-shirt. He only had three to his name but he would gladly relinquish one for the baby. First though, he had to make sure his idea would follow to its logical end. He put the sleeve openings around his neck and pulled the tail-end up to make a sturdy knot of the hem-line. Good. Now he had a pouch. He reached in with his fist, which was only slightly smaller than the bundle he planned to carry, and when he worked it all the way to the bottom, he realized that the material, though not heavy, bunched around his closed hand. Would she smother in there? He needed something to put in the bottom of the

34

shirt—something strong enough to keep it spread open and pliable enough so it would support the baby and keep her pretty much in one place. He didn't want her jostled around during the trip. He laughed softly to himself. The bible. He worked the bible that he and Eller had shared down into the material of the shirt the same way he had his fist, and found that it fit perfectly, making a neat, rounded square at the base where the edges of the book curved upward like a small hammock. He lifted the baby up from the ground where she still lay and looked into her face. *I reckon you goin to have a name fore we know if you'a live or die, little'un. I aim to name you.* Lige had never named a person before and did not take the task lightly but even so he knew he couldn't waste time. He recalled the blackness of her eyes and thought for a moment. What had eyes that black? Snake-eyes? Her eyes had reminded him of the two dots of the die when snake-eyes were rolled but knew no girl would want to be called Snake-Eyes. Naming a person was a big responsibility. What were those flowers Eller had at the house with the black middles? Yep, he had it. Black-eyed Susans. *Susan, that's who you are now. How do you like that, Susan?* The baby opened her eyes for the briefest of moments and Lige took that to be an affirmative response. *Well, come on Susan, we got to go!*

Lige patted the front of his overalls, making certain his bottle of shine was present and accounted for. It was. And then he remembered the bottles he aimed to take with him. How was he going to carry all of it down when he needed to travel as light and unencumbered as possible? The hell with the Shifflett boys, he didn't owe them any liquor. He didn't owe them anything. It was Danceray he owed and that was a debt he'd never be able to repay. He put the peach brandy in his left front pocket but seeing as how it was in a mason jar it took up so much space in the pocket that his pants snugged up around his leg. He unbuttoned the two buttons on that side and released the tension. Now if the jar didn't fall out on the way, he was in business and if it did, well, he just wouldn't mention bringing it in the first place. People never missed what they never had, did they? He breathed in, filling his lungs with fresh mountain air, and exhaled slowly, almost painfully releasing the breath. *Eller, I don't rightly know if you'll hear me this time but if you'll talk to God for me one more time, it'd be real good. He heared you last time and you give me the answer. Ast him to let me get this lil baby, Susan, down Pouter and up Salter safe. And ast him if'n he don't mind to let me come back the same way I left. I be thankin you kindly.*

Lige reckoned there was no better way to get this done than to get started and headed toward the path he'd worn on his way in and out of his camp but then he turned and walked back to the shelter. He went to the nightstand and opened the drawer, being careful not breath in the interior odor, the one that knocked him down yesterday. Was it only yesterday? He took out the calendar and made a mark with the carpenter's pencil. Thursday. And then he scrawled in his child-like handwriting, he wrote on the square representing the date, *Found Susan.* He replaced the calendar and took out the small handgun buried underneath the contents of the drawer. The gun, a Smith and Wesson was only a .22—a pea-shooter but even so, he felt much better with it than without it. After Papa Worley died, Lige asked Careen for the gun for at the time and at his age he believed it was a powerful weapon. Careen said that he certainly could have the gun but she wanted to put it away for him for a while, just until he was a little bit older, more mature. Careen, of all folks, should have understood that almost anything could be turned into a dangerous weapon but, perhaps, she figured that Lige was too innocent, too good-natured to come to know that on his own. As it turned out, he hadn't taken the gun until after Careen, herself, was dead and buried. But that was another thing he wasn't prepared to think on just yet. Now, he released the cylinder and made sure it was still loaded. It held five bullets. He turned the cylinder past the empty chamber insuring that there was a bullet in front of the hammer. He put the revolver in the back pocket of his overalls and his hand brushed against the other item he'd picked up at the landfill. The item he found on the bank near the dead girl. There was something about that item that pulled at the edges of his memory making him think he'd seen it before but he'd have to deal with it later. He had to hurry to Salter Ridge—to Danceray.

Chapter 5

Night traveling was easier in some respects but a body lost track of time in the dark. Familiar landmarks became foreboding and strange. Trees appeared taller and denser. The brush and brambles seemed full of secrets and hidden dangers. And the sounds of the night were almost savage and brutal. The screech of a hoot-owl turned into an ominous threat, the scampering of possums became footfalls of a dangerous follower, and the rasping of bat-wings grew into blood-sucking incubi in the imagination. The few times Lige dared to look to either side of the path, the staring eyes unnerved him so irreversibly that he resolved to keep his eyes directly on the path before him. He knew he overreacted and that any man of his size, and especially one with a gun, should have no cause for such fear but he was anxious, his nerves on edge.

He decided to whistle. He whistled every tune he could remember and then made a few up and before he knew it he was all the way down Pouter Mountain. And once his feet touched ground outside the tree-line in Mabry's Crossing he wondered where the time had gone. How did time play such tricks on a person? Sometimes it tightened until it seemed that the hour would never turn—the minutes frozen in some kind of warp that did not move forward or backward—and then there were other times when time loosened so much that the seconds whizzed into minutes that zipped into hours and the hours hurtled into a whole day of timelessness. Thinking this way made Lige's head hurt so he forced himself to think on another subject. The subject he'd avoided all the way down Pouter. Danceray. And then he stepped the first step on the path that he had steered clear of for an age of time. Now there was a time worth thinking of. How had years passed interminably, yet Lige didn't feel in his mind a minute older than that last time? Oh yes, his body felt the passage of time but in his wits and in his memory he was still that same young man who had not yet committed any act of violence, no blood had yet been spilled, no life taken, none given. He had just been a fresh faced, hopeful, expectant fellow with the same dreams that most of his ilk dreamt, the same purpose that made him want to awaken to each new day rested and eager to embrace whatever came his way. To persevere, but not only with the desire to keep at something with a stubborn, willful nature but to make an improvement on what has been done in the past, to advance and progress—to move forward, beyond all the efforts of others. To accomplish the one thing that all parents hope and fear their offspring will. To surpass, to exceed, their own best efforts. For to outdo and outshine means that the child has outgrown the parent and that is at once a positive and negative and these feelings are felt in equal measure by the grown child's same sex parent. Pride quickly and without control, and often without knowledge, turns to resentment. Lige had been that kind of man at one time, the time before the demons came. Before they goaded him from the fringes of his camp, before they haunted, tortured, him in his dreams, and most certainly long before he found the courage and strength to run at them screaming and hollering with all his soul in his throat and mouth. Before they tucked their tails and slithered into the darkness. He must at all costs keep them at bay. He cannot survive another time when he would be forced to look into their bloody mouths, recognizing the mangled pieces of flesh hanging between their teeth—waiting to devour him as they have done others.

Without even realizing that he did so, he reached to touch the baby, Susan, through the thin cloth of the tee-shirt. *God please let her live. Let me to do this thing right. Let me do good. Amen.* The bundle did not move and neither did it make a sound but it was still warm and her warmth was all he needed to hold out hope and possibility. He started up the second of four steep inclines toward the ridge. He was almost there. This slope and two more and he would be on Salter Ridge—face to face with Danceray. He was safe now. He could allow himself to finally permit the memory of Danceray to unfold from deep within the recesses of hidden, blocked recollection. But he would not, could not, let the reminiscence, the nostalgia of that time, especially the last time, come on strongly because to do so would mean that he would no longer be able to hold himself together. He would come apart and would then be no good to anyone. Not to himself and certainly not to Susan. He must remain strong, and intact. But he would think about it some; he could go a little ways down memory lane, just not too far. Not past a certain point. He would stop just before he got to the part that would undo him, unravel his sanity, he knew the point and he could cut it all off before he reached it. Of this he was a veritable genius. He stopped on the path and worked his hand down into the front pocket of his overalls and pulled out the bottle. He'd only had a few drinks while coming down the mountain. He was nowhere near drunk yet. Not even close. He took a huge guzzle of the shine, large even for him, and let the liquor rest at the back of his tongue for a brief pause before swallowing it, and then he took another, smaller drink. No sense in being a hog. He

40

replaced the bottle and when his fingers brushed against the fabric of the tee-shirt this time he felt Susan twist to the side toward his hand. He felt tears well up in his eyes. *She's alive. Thanks be to the Lord! Susan's alive. Don't you fret lil one we a be seein Danceray terectly. She'a know what needs doin.* Lige wiped at his eyes and moved on.

Lige consoled by the fact that the baby still lived and spurred on by the warmth of the shine and, he might as well admit it, he was feeling the glow of its effects too, opened up his mind but forced his heart to remain shut tightly. He would not, no matter what, open up his heart. Not again. Not ever. His heart had been closed for years and so it would remain. Lige's heart had no room for love. Not the love of a woman, a brother, a cousin, and no, not even a baby. All of those feelings were dead and by God they would stay dead. He would never consent to breaking down the barriers and walls he'd so painstakingly erected against tender emotion. Brick by mortared brick and board by nailed board had been erected against and across those feelings until it was impossible for them to resurface; they would never emerge, never spill over or out and seep under or between. And he was happy that way—content. But just this time, he would think of her and not instantly push the thought out of his mind. He would take out the memories one at a time until they became so painful that he could no longer think about them, and then he would lock them away again safe from him and anything he could do to manage to hurt her, to disappoint her.

Danceray, the woman he had loved first and hardest. Lige supposed that if any man had ever loved any woman harder than he did her then they would have both died from the force of that love. As dangerous as Lige's love for Danceray had been for any man to have exceeded

41

that kind and depth of emotion would have caused complete and utter destruction and eternal damnation. The thought of the love he felt for her then, now poured purely from his heart making it ache like molten lead. How could a body really feel the pain in an organ that had nothing whatsoever to do with sentiment or passion? The heart had no other purpose than to fill with blood and dump it back out. The heart was not the site of love, unrequited or fulfilled, not the location of arousement, and not the place of aching, yearning, burning devotion, but sure to God, he felt these sensations right there in the middle-left section of his chest. And they were as real and tangible as they were elusive and intangible. How could he explain how he felt even to himself who on some level already knew but did not comprehend? All he need do was think of her and though he could not hold those feelings in his hands he could feel them in his being as if they sat there above his ribs, a weight that he truly could hold. If he could only once remove them from inside of himself, this creature that he was, would his weight in fact, be reduced by the ridding of the mass? And if so, how much would it weigh? Would there be any left of him? Would he cease to be Lige Worley? He was not sure he would know how to be him if he were to find himself without that piece of love for her that he'd carried with him all of these years. Eller came to the front of his mind and for a moment he felt guilty but then he reasoned that Eller hadn't loved him either, not really anyway. Eller had had her eye and heart set on someone else the whole time but her hopes and desires went unfulfilled just as had his own.

He knew how she felt and could say with certainty who she deep down inside loved because they all had been a close-knit bunch. Some of them had been, and still were in the strictest sense of the word, family, and some had been friends. A few of them had grown into enemies, while others had been enemies from the start, inheriting those feelings from way back through previous generations. But they each knew the hearts of the others—sometimes, in some cases—better than their own. When Lige allowed himself to be completely honest where Danceray was concerned, he had to admit that he'd loved her since—well, since always. Always before and always since; there had never been a time in his life when he hadn't been in love with Danceray Woodruff. Eller had loved Rooster or she believed she did. Rooster Shifflett, Lige's cousin and Clayton and Tater's middle brother. Lige chastised himself for doubting Eller's love for Rooster, admitting that casting a shadow on her feelings came only from his wounded manhood, the kind of masculinity that could accept that he loved another but that his wife could not. Of course, she loved Rooster, for hadn't he seen her make her way down to the creek-bed that day in Mabry's Crossing when Rooster put the wedding band on Danceray's hand and they afterward kissed for the first time as man and wife. And hadn't he, feeling the same way as she, when the kiss sealed the sacrament between the one Lige loved and the one Eller loved, followed her down to sit beside her on the bank, neither talking and neither wanting to believe their hopes had so easily and unalterably been dashed. Finally, Lige reached out and took her hand in his, patting it ever so softly, and after a few last moments of wishing what was so wasn't so she turned to face him, not crying exactly but he saw the tears that had been cut short by her sheer strength of force clinging wetly to her lashes. She turned to him and nodded once in downward direction. She firmly grasped the hand that held hers and pulled herself up from where she sat, and, though the pact between them was unspoken, somehow they understood that from that moment forward they would be together. They two, who were perhaps the only ones who could understand and accept each other, knowing what they knew.

Now, he stood on the highest point on Salter Ridge. Nothing had changed except the trees had grown taller and fatter and the underbrush thicker and wider. The same two paths still led in the same two directions. They lay ahead of him sprawled out like an upside-down dousing rod. He knew that the path to the right led him to Danceray's house and the path to the left would take him to Tater's. Lige peeped into the sling of the tee-shirt, trying to determine how Susan fared but she made no sounds and showed no effort at movement. *Please God, let Susan be okay. Eller, tell God to let her be okay. Amen.* He started down the right path headed to Danceray. The moon was full and the stars hung so low he fancied he could reach right up and grab one like a big, fat apple. The night sounds and shapes were no longer trepiditious; in fact, they beckoned to him now when before coming down Pouter they'd practically chased him, breathing on him with huge hot puffs of breath, scalding his skin and prodding him forward with giant hooked claws. Here, the spirits were friendly, welcoming. He heard the crickets and katydids sing-songing him along. *Step-skip. Step-skip. Step-skip. Almost there. Almost there. Maybe one more mile. Maybe less. Step-skip. Step-skip. Step-skip.*

Almost before he was ready, though his heart had been ready for years, her house was in sight. His breath caught deep in his chest and would move no further up into his esophagus, nor his flattened wind-pipe, until he remembered to breathe. He had to consciously move the breath upward and out and as he exhaled he, for the first time that evening, wondered how he looked. For the first time, in fact, for years, he wondered about his appearance. He reached up and smoothed back his hair, licking the ends of his fingertips to make it stand down at the sides. He felt his long, grizzled beard and wished he had taken time to shave. But there had been no time for that. He glanced down at his belly, the paunch of it making him appear to be a might older than he was. And then he wondered about Danceray. Had she changed too over the years? Perhaps she too had begun to find gray hairs in her silky, dark hair. Maybe there were a few wrinkles at the edges of her eyes from staring at the sun, or laughing like she always loved to do. Had her throat and jaw-line begun to sag just a little? Always before, though he had grown older and lost muscle and tone over the years, he imagined Danceray looked just as she had the last time he'd laid eyes on her. That, however, was impossible. Everyone aged. No one was exempt from the ravages of time. Lige was certain that even though she would show some signs of age, she'd grown into a better person for that was Danceray's way. Nothing and no one could hold her down or back. Danceray was everything in the universe that was vibrant, intoxicating and alive. Danceray would never fall victim to discouragement or despondency. She could and would survive anything and everything.

He paused in front of her door with his hand raised, prepared to knock on the wood. *What do I say to her? What can I say?* He could wait no longer and he watched as his hand rapped on the door almost without his awareness of having told it to. There were no lights on inside. Maybe no one had heard him knocking. He beat on the door a little more in earnest. He watched through the window as a lamp in the living room came on illuminating only the far end of the room, and then he heard footsteps. Small feet. Danceray's feet. The door opened a slight wedge, almost but not quite large enough to fit his hand through. Of course, he wouldn't be so bold to reach inside her door even if she slammed it in his face. His heart pounded and his lips and tongue lost all moisture. The clock inside his body hummed and tick-tocked until he believed he might have been standing there on her step for all the years he'd been absent from her, waiting for her to open the door. *Just open the door, Danceray. Just open the door and let me look at you! Open the door. Please.* Almost as if she heard the prayer of his heart, she opened the door wide. He took in the surprise and beauty of her face and his chest wanted to burst wide open—as wide as the door. As wide as the sky above them.

"Elijah," she said.

Just the one word, *Elijah*. He hadn't heard his full name pass the lips of a woman in such a very long time and for the briefest moment he believed he might spill tears but he caught them before they came. He couldn't cry now. Not in front of her, especially. He opened his mouth to speak but before he could form a thought from feeling, before he could make a sound, she reached out as fast as a striking rattlesnake and slapped his face with all her might. And though she was still a small woman she was a strong one.

Chapter 6

Blacky Jackson almost never slept and when he did he struggled with short naps. Sometimes two hours, once in a while he might get three hours in a row. He hated these fucking mountains and as soon as he could he was going to make his way back down this one and head on back to the Everglades. Back to the flatlands and the ocean. As he leaned against a tall pine, up on Pinter Mountain, Pinter— what the hell kind of name was that, anyway?—he watched the buckra daddy and his boy sleeping—their faces slack, mouths slobbering. These white people made him sick. Nasty is what they were. He'd been out here with them for three days engaging in their idea of hunting and he hadn't seen either wash one face or ass between them the whole time. They eat with dirty hands. They chew tobacco and spit the brown, slimy juice back out it in huge globs of saliva and snot right on the ground. Tater? What kind of grown man goes by a name like Tater? He figured if his name was Eustus he would call himself something else too, but certainly not Tater. He was so filled with contempt for these two men that he often over the past week thought about just running them through the blade of his knife. But because Eustus Jr. had been so kind to help him out of the mess he got himself into down in Florida, he knew that he must ignore these murderous urges out of loyalty if nothing else. The kid had walked out of that bar with him and rode him out of there in his old Chevy pick-up and they laid rubber all the way from the Glades to these mountains somewhere in either North Carolina or Tennessee, he wasn't sure which. Maybe it was both. Seemed like one minute he was in one state and the next he was in the other. Maybe it was neither. In fact, he was terribly confused and couldn't get his bearings where geography was concerned. Before now, he'd never even seen a real mountain. The way they twisted and turned and unwound both upon themselves and neighboring ones made him feel like a giant child playing a game of Blind Man's Bluff. His internal compass was so agitated that for the most part he couldn't determine north from south. East and west was a little easier because of the sunrise and set but sometimes up here even the sun was difficult to locate. And he couldn't lie, not to himself, he could to the others, but he felt entirely claustrophobic in these hills. The trees were in his way like thick bangs covering a wide forehead. He wanted to brush them aside so he could see the horizon. Sure, they had their majestic qualities. Sometimes when he rounded a bend and came upon a ridge overlooking the world below and beyond, his breath caught in his throat and he felt the beauty deep in his heart, but just as soon as his eyes took in those images Tater and Eustus Jr. were ready to move on for they'd seen these hills and mountains and valleys for a lifetime and like anything so familiar the scenery had long ago lost its allure. They were like a fine-looking woman who once had one has come to take for granted. But there was one huge benefit to these mountains. Though he still didn't sleep well or long he slept better and harder. The air was thinner, with less oxygen so he was more often able to drift off. Once in a while, he even had a dream or two too.

Another thing for sure was that his people just didn't live this way. Everything's so difficult here. He came from hearty Gullah and Seminole stock—a group that came to be known as Black Seminoles. His first American ancestor, along with several others, escaped from a rice plantation down in St. Helena Island in South Carolina and made their way to Florida after banding together with others from South Carolina and Georgia. They took to and prospered in the Everglades and the surrounding areas because the terrain, flora and fauna were so similar to their homeland in Africa. They eventually fought long and hard against the buckras to keep their land and to live free. His people were noble, proud and clean and almost impossible to beat in a fair fight. They made intricate fishing nets the same way African people had always made them and lived on the high protein of seafood. These people have to work too hard to hunt down the animal flesh they eat. And some of the animals he couldn't even recognize. And the food wasn't tasty in his opinion. Too much grease and too much starch and too damned many beans. In fact, eating their food had caused him an almost unceasing stomach gripe and flatulence. These buckras eat the food like it's manna from heaven, sometimes picking up chunks of meat with their fingers, allowing the grease to drip down their chins into their beards and then the pieces they couldn't pick up easily were *sopped up* with large chunks of bread they called pones. One night Tater's wife cooked what he could swear he thought she said was a possum and he'd watched her, while he stood on the back porch smoking a cigarette, go down to the bottom of the yard and collect greens that she called *poke salet*. She told him that they had to be washed three times and then cooked. The pot liquor was then poured off, the greens washed again and cooked one final time to keep them from being poisonous. He'd gone hungry that night, not even caring that he might be considered rude. If he was going to die, he would die in the glades where they could bury him properly.

49

One other thing he had noticed about these people was that they ran hot and cold—no warm. They were all in or all out. There was no in between with them, no middle ground. And sometimes, most times, a stranger had no way of telling which way they were headed where temperament was concerned. He, Blacky, stayed pretty much even-tempered as far as he could tell with any kind of self-evaluation. It was true that he could be a moody bastard but he didn't often lash out at others. Now, that's not to say he wouldn't take care of business when it was called for—he just wasn't guilty of grinning from ear to ear one moment and cutting someone from ear to ear the next. If Ol' Black Jack came for you, then you knew what was going down. No tricks about any of it. No sneakiness. These people were tricky bastards. He didn't trust them— not one bit. And after what he saw Tater do to that little pregnant girl, the faster he got away from them and here, the better. He did wonder too what happened to the baby. How long did it take it to die? How much did it suffer? Did a baby still attached to its mama like that drown in fluid, suffocate without air, or did the lights just go out for it? Maybe it didn't hurt that baby, after all. He hoped it didn't, anyway. He was no saint and he wouldn't try to make himself out to be one. He'd gotten into plenty of scrapes and a couple of them had led to somebody's dying but he ain't ever killed a woman or a baby. No, that kind of deed wasn't for him. It just wasn't his way.

The sun was coming up somewhere, he knew because he saw the ground lightening up first in a few mottled, dappled places and then the light began to make its way up from the bottoms of the surrounding trees. Seemed to him that this was backward but hell everything seemed like that these past few days. He heard a bird

50

singing in the not too far distance. The creature's song was unfamiliar to him for he didn't know the sounds of nature in this part of the world. He could tell, however, from the tone and melody that it came from a small song-bird. He felt, rather than saw, Tater stir and when he turned his gaze to the man he saw him wipe the drool from the side of his face and beard and wipe his dirtied hand on his trousers and then wipe and scratch at his eyes with the butts of both of his hands. Tater stretched and yawned with his mouth agape showing the cavernous hole all the way to the throat and Blacky saw that he was missing quite a few of his teeth in the back and along the sides. No wonder his cheeks always appeared sunken. But when Blacky took in Tater's whole face and posture he realized that he was as content and rested as if he'd just awakened in a king-sized bed awaiting room service in a fancy hotel. Tater's hair was still black as a boot and his eyes, almost as black, were bright and lively but there was a cruelty in him that Blacky didn't see as human. He was full of spirit but no soul. When Blacky looked the man in the eyes he saw nothing behind them. A couple times, he'd been startled to see his own reflection doubled and staring back at him. Tater's eyes took everything in while allowing nothing out. He was an absorbent sponge, draining and retaining every ounce of life he could suck from others but never, never leaking any of himself, never replenishing the energy he greedily took. And he was not only stingy with his emotions, thoughts, feelings, but also with things. And— not only his possessions and belongings but yours as well. If he has a cigarette, then he wants yours too; if he has a woman, then he wants yours too; if he has a thing that he cannot even name, then he wants your nameless item too. As Blacky continued to appraise him, Tater picked up a dirt clod and threw it at Eustus Jr. who fell over face first on the ground and raised his head slowly, carefully checking his surroundings.

"Wek up, Junior! Time to rise an shine!"

"You scared the shit outta me, Daddy!"

The younger man scrambled up from the ground, retrieved his hat and shoved it on his bullet-shaped head. Having none of his father's good-looks, he was an ugly fellow but he was also lacking his father's pitiless brutality, which might in his case allow him to come out on the winning end at the finish. Now, his sister, Miranda, she was a different story, entirely different from her brother in looks and while she didn't appear to be malicious she did show signs of a respectable feistiness. He smiled, thinking that she just might be the only thing that could keep him in these mountains. He wondered if she would consider coming down off Salter Ridge and going back to Florida with him. Staying away from the police down home and Miranda might just be enough to make this hell-trip worth it as far as he was concerned. He realized that this was not the first time he'd thought of Miranda this way but for some reason it was the first time the thought had become so important to him. He felt the blood rush to his penis and the front of his trousers rise in an intense erection. He felt Tater and Eustus Jr's gaze and smiled.

"Go'n get rid a that piss hard-on. Ain't no room for it twixt the three of us," Tater said.

Chapter 7

Lige stood in the doorway of Danceray's house, his mouth
wide and slack, his face stinging with the burn of the palm
of her tiny hand, and his heart near bursting with love and
a multitude of other emotions—some of which he could
name, others he could not. There were two things he
knew at that moment. One, Danceray stood before him.
Danceray, who for so long had lived only in his heart and
memory. But then, that was nowhere near the truth for
she had been sole inhabitant of his soul. And two, he held
this baby next to the warmth of his body—this little baby
who more than anyone needs to be taken care of, and he
didn't know how to do that by himself. And he knew too,
there was one more thing. He needed to speak up, needed
to say something and he was more afraid of actually
speaking to her than anything else in the world. *Screw up
your courage you ol' fart of a fool! Speak! What? What do
I say to her? After all this time and all my past.* But Lige
didn't have the luxury of self-examination at the moment.
Susan needed the nurturing hands and heart of a woman
and unless and until he was turned away, as far as he was
concerned she would have just that.

"Danceray," he began.

Lige's throat closed rendering his mouth dead as a
struck match. He swallowed hard and began again.

"Danceray. In this tee-shirt hangin round my neck
there's a tiny, infant child. Please don't turn us away.
Please. We need your help in a bad way. I think she's a
dyin."

Danceray's eyes widened and she took Lige by the arm and pulled him inside, closing the door behind them. Before she closed the door, however, Lige noticed she peered out, checking in all directions.

"Let me see the baby. Who's baby is it?"

Lige worked the tee-shirt from around his neck, carefully removed Susan from the top of the bible and carefully handed her off to Danceray, feeling as he did so a vast sense of relief and for the first time since he'd taken the child, a calm composure. She was in Danceray's hands now and that meant she would be all right. That is if it were possible for her to be after all she'd been through so far. He wondered, not for the first time, what effects lying there on the ground of the creek-bank, still attached to her dead mama, might have on her health, her chance of survival. Silently and quickly, he prayed.

"Lige?"

"Huh? Oh. I don't know. I found her."

There was something in the depths of Danceray's eyes that he couldn't name, couldn't comprehend. Was it fear? No, not fear exactly. Perhaps it was caution. He just didn't recognize the look. Worry? Yeah. She was worried but there was more to her expression and demeanor than worry. He allowed his eyes to follow her around the front room and the connected kitchen area of the house. He watched her heat water in a small pot on the stove and as she removed stark, white bread-cloths from a drawer, throwing one over her left shoulder and laying the other flat out on the countertop. When she moved to the cabinet, his gaze followed her hands as she removed some powdered milk, and then when she rummaged in another drawer until she found a pair of blue, rubber gloves. She went back to the stove and set on another pot of water and then turned her attention once more to him and this time he recognized the fear, caution, worry and compassion in her eyes. And he saw her upper lip tremble and her chin quiver just before she quickly and emphatically brought them under her control. And once she did, he was left to wonder if he'd even seen what he'd thought. Had she been about to cry?

More than he believed it was possible to ever want, he wanted to hold her in his arms, to smooth her hair—the wayward wisps—away from her face, to take charge and tell her everything would be fine. He wanted to do these things but when he looked down at his large hands he saw them trembling, shaking with the very fear he sought to protect Danceray from.

"Lige, this baby's still covered in blood and fluid. It's God's wonder it ain't dead what with its throat not even cleared open. And my God! Is that hair? Is it? Is it hair?"

"Yeah, it's hair."

"What have you done now? What have you done!"

Lige knew she was right to suspect him. There wasn't anything, in her opinion, any horrible act he wasn't capable of. To her, he was wicked. A scourge that had blighted her life in such an irreversible way that he could never be forgiven. He had ruined her life and he could never make it right; he could never take it back; he could never, he could just never. That was all. For him, as far as she was concerned, everything was never. Never and always at once. And that was an awful place to find oneself in—awful and irrevocable. He knew that even though he was right and she was right, there was no time to discuss the past right now. Now, Susan was the important consideration.

"I didn't do nothin, Danceray. I swear it. I found her. And this."

From his back pocket, Lige took the item he'd found near the dead girl's body—the third thing he'd carried with him back up the mountain—and handed it to Danceray. Danceray dropped the plastic gloves into the larger of the two pots of boiling water and removed the smaller pot from the heat of the burner and set it on a trivet. Lige was bothered by the fact that she didn't answer him. He couldn't decide if she believed him or not and it was important to him that she did. Even with all of his faults, even with all he'd done in the past, he would never hurt a child or a woman. Not on purpose anyway. He watched her moving in the kitchen, wondering what she was doing. How was all of this going to help Susan? The powdered milk made sense, but all this boiled water and cleaning gloves. Danceray worked quickly, ignoring his presence as she moved back and forth between Susan and the stove. She dipped one of the breadcloths into to the warming water from the pot on the trivet. She scrubbed furiously at Susan's skin, working from head to toe. Lige noticed that something was coming off the baby's skin that looked like rolled up pieces of cheese. He didn't like looking at all this but as he watched the process closely he saw her skin turn bright red and purple in some places, and she finally let out a howl. Lige stepped forward; he could stand it no longer. Danceray was hurting her and he would put a stop to it, even if it meant going against the woman he trusted above all others. He wouldn't abide her hurting this child.

"Danceray . . ." he began.

She held her hand up toward him palm out, indicating that she knew what she was doing.

"But she's hurtin."

"No, Lige. She's finally breathin right. Her throat was full of snot and fluid. It's God's wonder she ain't dead as long as it took you to get up the ridge with her. She's a strong-un."

"But you're rubbin her skin so hard it's red."

"It's gettin her blood goin through the veins. And it's gettin her clean. She was a nasty little thing!"

"You sure?"

"Sure about what?"

"You sure about it bein what she needs?"

"Positive sure."

For the first time since she'd opened the door that evening, she smiled. She wrapped Susan in another of the breadcloths and handed her to him. He took her roughly and held her up against his body, waiting to be told what to do next.

"I have to find her some clothes. She can't go around naked. But first you feed her."

"Feed her what?"

Again she held up her hand; this time signifying that she had everything under control.

"Sit down in that chair over yonder."

Lige sat down in the chair she pointed to and waited. Danceray took one of the gloves from the water that still boiled on the stove and laid the glove on a new cloth. She took down a mason jar from a tall cabinet and poured out some of the powdered milk into the jar. Lige watched her pour some warmed water into the jar and then shake it vigorously mixing the contents thoroughly. But what she did next, he considered a stroke of genius. He'd come to the right place—to the right person—that was two sure things. She picked up the glove and through the opening poured a few ounces into it holding the glove tilted so that the milk mixture travelled primarily down into the rubber, index finger. Next she located a large, darning needle and holding it by the eye with a pot-holder against the still red-hot burner, sterilized it. She then worked the needle through the tip of the milk-engorged finger of the glove making an opening large enough for the baby to suckle. Lige felt hot tears well into his eyes but he blinked hard making them retreat. He would not cry.

Danceray handed him the make-shift bottle and after instructing him on how to properly feed the baby, she went into another room for clothing. Lige did as he was told, holding the glove just so, and as he watched Susan working hard to suck on the rubber finger he fell so hard in love with her that his heart beat in that time only for the tiny body he held in the crook of his arm. The body that was almost no larger than the palm of his hand. And without even knowing where the thought came from or whether there was any logical reason for it, he knew that he would kill, maim and dismember any human or animal that ever laid a finger on her or blew a breath of danger in her direction. To tear such a person limb from limb would appear to be child's play. He was full with sentiment and while Danceray was no longer in the room he did allow the tears to fall. There were only a few of them because when a person was as out of practice at crying as he the tears were hesitant. The pump not having been primed produced only a doubtful, jerky start and then a sputtering of an end. Susan flinched when one of the drops splashed onto her miniature forehead and with his free hand he wiped away the others. He wiped them from his face but his memory kept them, holding them tightly. He wanted these tears. He never wanted to forget them because they were, perhaps, the purest ones he'd ever shed. And they just might be the ones to eventually save him. They may just be the proof of his humanity.

Danceray came into the room just as the baby stopped drinking the milk and Lige, not knowing what to do next held Susan up to her. She took the baby from him and showed him how to burp her, explaining why the process was so important.

"Why're you showin me all this? Ain't *you* keepin her?"

Danceray stared gravely into his eyes before speaking. Lige was unnerved by the seriousness of her gaze and shifted uncomfortably in his chair.

"Well, ain't you?"

"No. You got to take her back with you."

"Danceray! I don't know nothin about babies. I ain't never even been around any. I'm . . . I'm a man, for God's sake!"

"Okay Lige. You got to listen to me and listen good. This is important. You say you found this here baby? Where's the mama?"

"She's layin in the landfill over on the creek-bed dead as a rung bell!"

"Um-hmm. That's about what I thought. Now here's where you listenin comes in. That pocketwatch you just handed me—it's Eustus Jr.'s. I know because I gave it to him several years ago, Christmas. Somehow the Shifflett's are involved with all this. Whether it's Eustus Jr. or Tater I don't know but I do know Eustus Jr. ain't the kind of boy to go killin nobody. If it's Tater and finds the baby she's likely to be the next one dead. And they'll be after you too. Because if'n you got Susan then that'll mean you know about the murder. You'll be a witness. You got to hide her. Take care of her. You hear me?"

Lige wanted to scream. The last thing he needed was to tangle with Tater Shifflett. He thought he was finished with him years ago. The last time he was over on this ridge. Fuck! Damn-it all to hell! And then he recalled how only a few moments ago he'd vowed, even if the vow was only to himself, to protect this baby—and somehow he believed that Susan knew about his vow. By some means, she was in on it the same way she would have been had they made a pact. She'd been baptized with his teardrop.

"I hear you. But I don't know how to take care of her. I can protect her but I don't know about all the other stuff. I mean, I ain't never even changed a diaper."

"I'm goin to show you all that. And then you get on back down this ridge before the sun comes up."

Lige didn't answer her right away. He didn't believe that there was anything, any request, any demand or desire, he could deny her. But this? Sweet Jesus, how had he come upon all this? All this over a damned ashtray! But then if it hadn't been for that ashtray, Susan would be dead by now and he couldn't abide the thought of that.

"Lige Worley! I didn't want to say this but you owe me. You put a axe in Rooster's head. Split it open like a summer melon. And when you done that you took my husband from me. But that ain't the worst of it. When you done that you took all my babies from me too. True, there won't no babies then but I had some to come and when you done what you done, you took him, takin them too. You understand me?"

"Yeah, I do."

"Now. This here baby, I know for a fact she's connected to Tater some way but I ain't figured the whole thing out yet. I aim to though. And when I do I'll tell you how. But I aim to have this baby in the end of it. I aim to have her. You hear me?"

This time when Danceray's upper lip trembled and her chin quivered, she let the tears come. She allowed them to make their way down her face and fall from the line of her jaw and it was clear she was unashamed to cry. Lige, relieved that the horror of his past deed finally lay

61

out in the open between them, stood and faced her. The fact that he killed Rooster was right there, linking, connecting them just as surely as if they held hands, embraced, coupled. The fact was almost a tangible, living, breathing entity. He moved, heart first, toward her. When he stood close enough to her to taste her breath, he spoke.

"Danceray. I'm sorry for the pain and loneliness I caused you. I am. But I ain't the kind a man to let things go. I don't let go easy. When I come up here that day and seen the bruises on your face—the face I loved, the face I love—and I seen how you couldn't barely walk from another beatin, I couldn't hardly see straight. Everything in me went wild and I seen him out there grinnin like a mule eatin briars. Next thing I knowed I had that axe-handle in my hand and it was done. It was done and over before I even knowed I hefted the weight. I can't take it back. I think I would if I could but I ain't sure about that. I ain't. Not down to the bone sure."

"Lige. Sweet Elijah. I ain't never been mad you did it. I hated him almost as fast as I loved him. I just wanted me some babies. You know, that's the onliest thing I missed. Well, that ain't the whole truth but I reckon the whole truth ain't so important no more."

Lige took her in his arms being careful not to lean too hard against the baby. He didn't know how to measure the length of their embrace. To him, time had become an absurd contradiction, something not to be trusted, and he didn't want to trust it as it stretched out to feel illogically like an eternal, blissful occasion. As long as Danceray was in his arms, he was content to allow time to roam, meandering its way to infinity. But then, traitorous time bent backward and bowed down upon itself, rapidly pushing the meaning of instantaneousness into and against his brain as she pulled away from him, breaking the hold of his strong arms. Lige felt his head spin slightly as he regained his weight without her body against his. When she stepped back, he saw a tenderness in her eyes that he had not seen since their youth. And when she reached to touch his face, his hand immediately moved to cover hers. And whether true or false, he believed that he made yet another pact that evening and these two above all other agreements were the most important ones of his life. They were to him, sacramental. They were of apologetic atonement but they were also of promise and pledge. He would not, under any circumstance, disappoint these two females because whether they ever knew or agreed they belonged to him.

Chapter 8

Just before sunrise the next morning, Lige hurried down Salter Ridge carrying Susan and all of the items that Danceray had sent for the baby's care in a picnic basket. So far, the baby had been a quiet child, not even crying much when she was hungry or soiled her diaper. She also slept a great deal. Danceray said that babies that new needed more sleep than anything else, explaining that just as animals grew during rest, so did humans. The human animal. So many similarities, so few differences between them. He made it down the ridge and into Mabry's Crossing even before any of the stores or cafes opened for business. He needed diapers. Danceray had sent cloth to use but they both agreed that he wouldn't be the best at keeping them clean. He wanted the throw-aways. He thought it might be a good idea to check with the Goodwill to see what kind of clothing and supplies they might offer. He knew though that it would be unwise to appear to be setting up housekeeping with a baby and neither did he need to go walking into the stores with Susan in tow. He sat down on a metal picnic table bench and carefully placed the basket on the top of the table just to his right. He needed to think. And count his money. He had the money for what he needed to put together his next batch of shine but that was still tucked away safe up on Pouter. He pulled out his change purse and poured the contents of silver and copper into his outsized palm. He counted two fifty cent pieces, three Susan B. Anthony dollars, nine quarters, twelve dimes, eight nickels and fourteen pennies. A little over eight dollars. How much did diapers even cost? How the hell would he know?

He glanced over to the tree-line just outside the path he took to the top of Pouter Mountain and home. He would just have to stash Susan to the side of the path up under the brush. He needed another him, another Lige. There was no way he could see for him to take care of her alone. But he knew even as he had the thought that there would be no other person. Ever since Eller and the baby died, he'd been alone. Oh God, he hoped Eller hadn't seen how he'd acted around Danceray. Had she been watching from heaven? Did she see his heart fluttering under the flesh of his chest? Was she jealous? He was just thinking stupid thoughts now, he knew, because although he was certain she'd loved him and he'd loved her too, they had always only given each other the love that had been left-over. The bits and pieces of love that had found a way to survive after they had each suffered the greatest heartbreaks possible after the words *I do* had tripped across the lips of Rooster and Danceray. How might their four lives been different if Eller had been the one to marry Rooster and Lige, Danceray? One thing he knew for a certain fact, and that was that Eller would never have taken the beatings that Danceray did. Make no mistake, Danceray was a strong woman but she was unable to fight the way Eller could. Danceray had never had to fight. Not for any reason. And, if the truth was told, Eller had had to fight for every single thing she got and every single thing she didn't get. If Rooster had ever once struck Eller, Lige would bet everything he had and half of what he didn't that she would have gotten him back before the next morning—somehow, someway.

Eller's mama was the same way. They all knew about the times she got back at Eller's daddy, Hamp. Lige laughed softly at the memories. One time had it that

Hamp had come in late. He'd been playing poker down at Pete's Place and drinking with the regulars and the story was he'd lost about all the money he had on him. Anyway, he came in through the back door, stomping his feet on the rug before entering the kitchen. Peggy had a stove full of food she'd been keeping warm for him but he was in such ill spirits after the game he threw half of it in the sink and the other half across the kitchen floor, saying it wasn't fit for the pigs. Apparently Peggy made some comment that Hamp didn't take too kindly to and he walked over and slapped her hard across the face. She didn't say a word to him afterward. Peggy got straight up from the chair where she sat and cleaned up the mess he'd made and then went to sit in the front room, quietly darning socks and underwear, Hamp's included. Later, when Hamp went to bed, Peggy waited until she heard his heavy, even breathing peppered with rhythmic snoring and she went right into the bedroom, tied Hamp to the bedposts with nylon stockings and commenced to beating the hell out of him with an extension cord.

Another time, she called the police. Shortly after arriving on the scene, the police officer, Nelson, got another call. Lige heard that that time Nelson handcuffed Hamp to the staircase banister. Hamp, knowing what had happened the last time he'd been tied down, begged Nelson not to leave him alone with Peggy, to put him in the back of the patrol car and take him with him. Innocently, Nelson turned to Peggy and asked if she thought she'd be all right until he could return. She said as long as Hamp was cuffed she reckoned she would. As soon as Nelson pulled out onto the road in front of the house, Peggy beat Hamp with a curtain rod until he was able to grab the end of it and take it from her, after which point, she started throwing objects from all around the house at him until Nelson came back, finding Hamp holding the curtain rod and covered with cuts, welts and bruises. Nelson said that because of what he was able to piece together he had no choice but to arrest Peggy for domestic abuse. Hamp said, "Domestic abuse? Peggy ain't laid a hand on me! She ain't a goin outta here. No sir!" No, he didn't reckon Rooster would have ever even hit Eller once; she came from a different kind of stock than Danceray. Not better and not worse, just different.

Satisfied that Eller wasn't mad at him because she of all people understood how he felt, and besides, she was the one who sent him to Danceray for help with the baby in the first place, Lige situated Susan along the path under the brush and made his way back out into the sunlight that by this time was full-up. He glanced at the Dollar General and then over to the Steak-N-Egg. He sure could use a cup of coffee. Danceray had cooked him a good breakfast before he had started out early that morning but after his trek down Salter Ridge he wanted three things. The first, he pulled from his pocket, uncapped and filled his gut with the fire of shine. He needed that drink about as badly as he had ever needed anything in his life. He wanted to retrace the previous events from the moment Danceray had opened the door to him last night—yes, even the force of the slap to his face—until she'd closed it behind him before daylight this morning but he knew that until he was alone and back at his shelter he would not be able to give them his proper attention. The other two wants he had at the moment was a cup of coffee and a large glass of water—maybe two. He wiped his forehead with the bandana he carried in his back pocket and made his way across the street to the Steak-N-Egg.

At the counter he ordered black coffee and ice-water. He drained the water and asked for a refill in less time than it took for the waitress to turn her back to him. She popped her chewing gum, rolled her eyes, and picked up the water glass while he checked the heat of the coffee with a tentative sip. There were already several tables filled with couples, one or two with only a single diner, and there were a few stray men sitting at the counter where he sat. And though he did not consciously attempt to eavesdrop, he overheard snatches of conversations that to him sounded very much like a radio between stations— where it's possible to hear more than one station at once. *Dead. Pregnant. Landfill. Strangled. Baby. Missing. Cord. Cut. Murder. Kidnapped. Police. Manhunt. Evil. Nobody. Safe. Dead. Dead. Dead.* Lige was certain there was more. There had to have been more said than that. He felt like a child with puzzle pieces spread out before him. If he put all of those words he overheard together what would they say? Exactly. In what order did they go? Maybe he should strike up a conversation with one or two of the men at the counter. Or maybe ask the waitress. Maybe he should keep his mouth shut and his curiosity too. But then, he had a lot riding on what was being said here, didn't he? Susan had a lot riding on it. And hadn't he promised Danceray? Given her his word that he would take care of this baby no matter what. He had also promised himself that he would protect Susan at all costs. He glanced down the counter and saw mostly unfamiliar faces but he thought he knew the one nearest to where he sat. What was that boy's name? Who was his daddy? He must have been staring at him because after a minute or so the boy looked at him with a raised eyebrow, questioning him without speaking. The boy had a tattoo on his upper arm of a colorful snake, mouth wide open but instead of eating a mouse the snake's mouth held a naked woman. He had to admit that even though the tattoo was in some way disturbing, it was also fascinatingly attractive.

"You got some'um to say old man?"

"Yeah. I know you from somewhere. Who's your daddy?"

"Ain't none a your god-damn business who my daddy is. Who's your daddy?"

"I don't know my daddy," Lige lied, "but I think I know yourn. He Ray Cleveland?"

"Depends on who wants to know. He might be. Might not be."

"I got it now. Ray Cleveland. Lives over by the river."

"*Used* to live over by the river. *Buried* over by the river now."

"Sorry to hear that. He was a good man. Last time I seen you though you had no front teeth and a nose full o'snot. Must a been seven or eight."

The young man clicked his tongue under a gum-colored retainer and released two false teeth from his mouth, and laughed.

"Grew them two back and got the sum-bitches knocked out again. Some thangs never change, do they old man?"

"I ain't that old a man. You get my age, if'n you do, you'll feel full a piss and sperm still, watch and see."

"I hope so. I sure do."

Lige watched him soaking up egg yolk with a square of toast and silently tried out a couple ways to approach the subject of the dead girl. Finally, he decided just to plunge right in. That seemed to be the way everyone else was discussing it anyway.

"Hey, what's all this about a dead girl?"

"They found a dead girl at the dump last night."

Lige thought of the girl he'd seen out there yesterday, Susan and the horrible sight of the umbilical cord. He wanted to vomit but grimaced and swallowed hard to keep from it.

"And a baby?"

"No. Now that's what's so fucked up. There was a baby but somebody took it. Bet it was the killer what done it."

"You think the killer took the baby? What makes you think there was a killer anyway? Couldn't she a killed herself?"

"Strangled. You can't choke yourself to death—not from the outside. Has to be murder!"

"They got anybody in mind?"

"I heared her mama said she was seein some old man."

"You got something goin with the old man thing, don't you?"

"No. I'm serious man. He musta been as old as you."

"How old was the girl?"

"A few years behind me in school. I reckon. twenty-two, twenty-three maybe."

"You said her mama said she was seein somebody. They know who the girl was?

"Of course. Everybody knowed Rhonda. Good girl. Didn't deserve what she got that's for sure."

Oh shit! That means Susan has a grandmother. He hadn't even thought about anything like that. Well, it didn't matter what kind of family she had, they weren't getting her. The baby belonged to him. He found her; he saved her; she was his. Period.

"They sayin why they think the killer took the baby?"

"Where the hell else would the baby be, man?"

"Don't know. How would I know? Just don't make no sense."

"Nope. No sense at all."

"Well, good talkin to you."

"Yeah."

Lige paid his tab and walked back outside. He stood thinking in the parking lot of the Steak-N-Egg. He needed another snort of shine. How in the hell was he going to walk into the Dollar General and buy diapers now that everybody knew there was a missing baby? No way was that going to happen. He'd just have to use those cloth pieces Danceray sent. Shit! Those cloth ones won't last a week and even if he washed them out in the creek, he'd be spending all his time just keeping them clean! Damn! He took another drink. And then another. And then he knew what he would do. Shine cleared the mind and blanked the sense. But even so, with a clarity that was rare for him he capped the bottle, put it back in his pocket and wiped the sweat from his face and neck with the bandana. Even he knew the sweat didn't come from the sun but from his nerves. He strode across the parking lots of the Steak-N-Egg and the Dollar General and entered the store with a purpose. He walked right up to a package of newborn diapers—ninety count—and opened the side, took out a handful and stuffed them in behind the front of his overalls. He picked up the package and took them back to the sleeping bags where he carefully wedged them in behind and toward the corner of the shelf. Then he went over to the food aisle grabbed a large jar of Peter Pan peanut butter and a large bag of jet-puffed marshmallows. For the first time, he wondered what it meant to be a jet-puffed marshmallow. What exactly was a jet-puff? He took the items to the front counter where a girl stood beside the register. She was flipping through a National Enquirer rag and did not immediately look up. Her head bent to read the headlines showed about an inch of dark hair at the scalp growing into the bottled blonde of the rest. He set the peanut butter and marshmallows down on the counter beside her magazine and she reluctantly set the paper to the side and began to ring up his purchases.

"You doin all right this mornin?"

"Yeah, I reckon. You?"

"I'm okay. Sleepy as hell. Nothin ever goin on in here this time a day."

"I heard some girl turned up dead. You know anything about that?" Lige said.

"Yeah. Everybody knows about it."

The cashier leaned forward, and conspiratorially said, "I went to school with her."

"Really? You friends?"

"Yeah and no. I mean everybody liked her but she didn't get too close to anybody. She stayed to herself most of the time."

"Wonder why somebody'd kill her?"

Lige figured anyone who would read and believe the National Enquirer would have an opinion on a local murder.

"Who knows why anybody kills anybody? But they say there's only a few reasons people kill people."

Lige glanced at her nametag and read the name Ivy spelled out in all capitols. IVY.

"What's the reasons?"

"Money. Sex. Power. And just plain meanness."

"Makes sense. Wonder which of them caused this one?"

"Well, since she was pregnant probably sex."

Ivy snorted like she believed the reason should be obvious and Lige needed to catch up. She dropped three pennies change into his shaking hand and he walked out of the store. He needed another drink but he would wait until he went back to Susan. What had he gotten himself into? He would turn this baby in to the police right then as shaken as he was if he hadn't promised Danceray. But even as he had the thought he knew that he was lying to himself. He already thought of Susan as his. His and Danceray's. He had never done one thing in his life that he thought was right and good but this time would be different. He had let everybody he'd ever been close to down but this time he wouldn't, he couldn't. He would do it right. And for the first time he realized that family was nothing but the people in your heart. No matter who the people were that you started with it was the ones you ended with that made up your family. And for him, now that Eller and their little baby were dead and gone—God bless them both—his family would be Susan and Danceray. Whether Susan and Danceray cared to have him as family or not didn't matter—their families could be different. They had the right to choose, just as he did. He turned off into the tree-line, located the picnic basket, opened the lid and peeped in. Susan was still asleep. God he hoped she was asleep. With all of the talk of death and murder, he felt the possibility that she had died too all alone under the brush and he stood watching her chest until he saw it almost imperceptibly move up and down once and then stop and then repeat the process. He took another drink from the bottle and wondered how and when he'd drank so much of the shine that the bottle was almost empty. He replaced the cap and put the bottle back in his pocket, picked up the basket and headed up the path. He needed to be back on top of Pouter before Susan woke up hungry. This would be the first time he did something for her without help. Other than saving her life and carrying her from the landfill, that is.

Chapter 9

Lige made it up Pouter in record time. He didn't know how he travelled faster than any other time before; he only knew that Susan's cries had given him a purpose he'd long been unfamiliar with. How long could an infant go without milk? What was the level of fragility with which he now dealt? The cries seemed urgent and the longer they went on the more pressing the situation appeared to be. Lige didn't know if she would just cry herself to death or not. Would all the crying hurt her? *Damn-it all to Hell! Danceray didn't tell me enough. This shit's serious business. What if I fail? What then? Susan could die and it'd be my fault. I could just stop right here an feed'er but Danceray said warm up the milk. I need water too.*

"Hush Little baby, hush now. Ain't no need for all this cryin."

The baby didn't hush. She cried harder and fiercer the closer they got to home. Home. Lige felt a new, fresh panic. Susan couldn't live under a tent. She needed a house. A house with walls, and rooms—a room of her own—and heat for the winter. How long before cold weather got here? There was no way around it; he'd have to build the house now. He'd start soon. And building a house meant money. Where would he get enough money to build a whole house? He needed some help. Not with the house. He could do that on his own. He needed some help with Susan. He couldn't just leave her alone while he gathered materials and supplies. Anything could happen to her up here alone. But he knew, too, that he couldn't take her with him. If anybody found out he had the baby all hell would break loose. Everybody believes the murderer took the baby. They would think he killed the girl, Rhonda. He would be arrested and he wouldn't have a story to tell about why it couldn't have been him. No alibi. No one would believe him. Thinking this way almost made him doubt himself. As much as he stayed drunk, he could have done anything and not even remembered doing it. But not murder. He couldn't murder a young pregnant girl, and besides he didn't even know her. He was being stupid, paranoid. He was shaky, nervous. And he was half drunk at the moment too. His mind had always been too strong for his own good and by that he didn't necessarily mean too smart, just too strong. He just had the ability to make anything real. He could talk himself into or out of anything and he didn't even know if that was a good quality or not. He spent too much time alone. And when a person's alone all of the time the demons came. They watched from the edges of sight—just where light ended and dark began. What did they want? What would make them happy, satisfied? If he knew the answer to that question, then he could give them whatever it was and be done with them. Or they would be done with him, more like. But he didn't know. No matter how many times he saw them, their eyes glowing red and white, their teeth shining, gnashing at him never moving forward nor receding away—always just sitting at the edges, waiting.

He quickly re-sparked the fire and poured the water into the pot, the one he used for grits, and heated it to just after warm and before the boil. He measured out the milk powder and poured the water into the glove on top of it. Then he closed his fist around the wrist of the glove and vigorously shook the contents to mix them thoroughly. He walked over to the shelter, picked up Susan and after guiding the finger of the glove to her eager mouth sat down with his back to the nightstand, allowing her to set her pace. He noticed that after a couple minutes of her sucking on the glove, a fine sheen of perspiration covered her tiny forehead. Were they supposed to sweat? He needed to write down all of his questions and as soon as he could he would go back to Danceray for answers.

Danceray would know. He believed he could take out his thoughts now and examine them one by one like items from a drawer. He closed his eyes and thought about the previous evening and into the early hours of the morning. About what they said to each other, about what they didn't say. He was relieved that he had been able to speak with her about Rooster's death—his murder. Lige thought about how strange it was that after all of these years and the two of them living so close, just down one mountain and up another with the only town for miles between them, they had never once ran into one another. People always talked about how it was a small world, remarked even how when folks would rather not see one another and took great lengths to avoid chance meetings, that their efforts were foiled because of the smallness of the world. There was a song about it—something about, *It's a Small World After all* and beyond those words he could only hum the rest. And yes, he supposed in many ways, in many instances, the world was small but where he and Danceray had been concerned the world was huge. And not only the world but even the small, insignificant area of the earth that the two of them inhabited. As far as he could tell, and truth to tell he didn't know much about the world outside of the hills and valleys of his part of the planet, the world was vast and great. When he pondered this concept in more detail, he wondered if wanting to see

78

another person, if needing to connect with that person, made the tie, no matter how deeply the desire was felt, even more tenuous. Almost as if the act of chasing, even if the chase was only in the confines of the mind and heart, caused the other to run away, even if running was also only confined by the same parameters. He wondered if at some point or points in the past he'd come out of a store in Mabry's Crossing and walked down a sidewalk where she'd just passed, or started up a sidewalk or into a store that she'd just come from. Had they crossed one another's paths, perhaps many times, and neither of them been aware? Or maybe Danceray had been and didn't want him to be. Maybe she had avoided him all of these years?

And if she had steered clear of him, had it been because he'd killed Rooster or was there another reason? When she said the words to him, he would have sworn under oath that he would never forget them. He would recall them perfectly because of the simple fact that they had come from her mouth, crossed her lips and they had been spoken to him but just as when one is awakened from a dream believing the content will be remembered later the words fell off the slate of his mind just as easily as if they were under the water at the crest of a waterfall, slipping over and down to be submersed once more in the water below. But he did recall the meaning of what she had said to him. She said that she had not been mad at him over Rooster's death. He felt once again the relief those words brought to him. Danceray had said more than that to him though. She said that the only regret she felt in her life was not having babies. She had expected babies and as a respectable married woman when her husband died she was unable to have them. For mountain folks some things were just simple that way. There had been something else hanging between them when she made the statement about the babies he'd taken from her in killing Rooster. What had she meant by it? She said something about there being one other thing she regretted but that it was no longer important. What did that mean? What had she meant by the comment? Had she realized that she left something so heavy hanging in the air between them? And how could something with such weight be suspended the way it had? Should he have asked about her other regret? Of course he should have asked her. What kind of fool allows a woman like Danceray to make a comment such as the one she made and not ask her? A fool like him does, that's what kind.

How many ways and how many times could he fail? And what's even more, how many times could he fail the woman he loved as much as he does her? Maybe his feelings for her were what caused him to never be up to snuff, to always fall short. Certainly, it was clear to him that the problem lay with him. Had she been trying to tell him in some delicate way that she regretted all the time and distance that lay between them? Even as the words were out rolling around in his mind, he felt foolish. Sure there had been a time when he knew Danceray loved him. She had said she did and he had had no reason to believe that she hadn't meant what she said. He had loved her too and he still loved her, would die loving her and hell he might even die of loving her but there had been a difference between her love for him and his love for her. Danceray betrayed him; he stayed loyal to her. He allowed his mind to travel down the road to the past twenty or so years, to recall the events that had forever changed four lives. He couldn't, however, permit himself to think about it all in detail. He may never be ready for all of the passion of feeling remembering everything would bring. Much of the past he realized should be left where it lay. No resurrection of it, no new breath breathed into it, no restoring it to life.

All of them had attended church picnics, hayrides, chicken stews, dances, movies and other social functions together. Lige and Danceray, though part of the group, often wandered away to be alone together. They talked of the future and he assumed they had been talking of the same future, a future for the two of them together. Actually, he knew they had. She had said so. They watched Rooster and Eller doing the same things, behaving the same ways and for the four of them everything seemed just right. Whenever all of them were together, the girls spoke of weddings and children and new quilting patterns. Once or twice, Lige and Rooster talked of the possibility of building their future homes close enough to allow for visits—dinners, card games, things like that. Abruptly and without explanation the whole lot changed. What once was fact without having been spoken the dynamics changed. Danceray and Rooster began to pair off in corners and even at dinner tables the two of them could be witnessed with heads bent closely together whispering and two or three times Lige heard Rooster laugh, almost a shrill girlish giggle, and when he turned his attention toward them he saw Rooster watching him, needing a reaction that he would not allow himself to give. During this time Lige and Eller had little choice but to turn to one another and in this kind of subtle, understated manner all of their lives took courses that none, with the exception, Lige believed, of Rooster, saw coming or had control over. True, Danceray probably had seen something in Rooster that had been absent in Lige but no one could argue, especially in hindsight, that that something was of superior quality. Neither Lige nor Eller had given up on the dreams and desires of their heart until the silence after the ringing of the church bells settled in their ears and souls. And if Lige was pressed to tell the truth about the way he and Eller felt, he would say that neither ever thought they would live the rest of their lives without their love eventually, finally, being fulfilled. That is, until Lige put the axe in Rooster's head and in some way or another ruined the lives of each of them.

He didn't know how long he'd been lost in thought when he looked down into Susan's face but what he saw frightened him. The baby's neck was elongated, stretched out over the crook of his arm; her mouth was slack with milk coursing down the side and down her chin to her neck. Her eyes were half-closed and he saw the eyeballs behind them flutter and move in such a way that he believed something drastic had happened. Susan appeared to be in the throes of complete mental failure. Lige leapt up from the ground carefully holding the baby, her head bobbing gently but surely, and stared wildly around him. What to do? What to do? He glanced over at his sleeping mat and decided it might be best to lay her down flat. He walked over and tenderly laid her down. He sat down beside her and watched as she twisted her body to the side making an almost perfect S shape, and opened her mouth in a huge, lusty yawn, then settled down peacefully. *Damn little-un! You scared me half t'death!* Lige laughed softly.

"I seen you take them Pampers!"

Lige whirled in the direction of the voice. How the hell had somebody sneaked up on him like that? He turned directly into the face of the girl from the Dollar General. Ivy. Fuck! Now somebody knew he had Susan. She was going to tell on him and then everything would be over and he knew for God's certainty he couldn't do one thing against her. He couldn't hurt her; he couldn't keep her quiet. He didn't have it in him. She wasn't like Rooster. The worst part right now though was that he had no idea what to say to her so he merely stared at her.

"I said I seen you take them Pampers."

"I heared you the first time."

"You killed Rhonda too didn't you?"

"No. I ain't killed nobody. And if you think I did what the hell you up here for?"

"Cause I ain't afraid of you or nobody else. And besides when you jumped up like you did I thought you already saw me. Figured I might as well come on out of the bushes."

"No. I didn't even know you was on the place. I thought something was wrong with Susan."

"She looks all right to me. What's wrong with her?"

"I don't reckon nothin is. I just ain't used to younguns."

"You goin to kill me now?"

"No. I ain't goin to kill you now. Or never."

"You sure you didn't kill Rhonda?"

"Yes, I'm sure. I saw her layin there dead though. The baby, Susan, was still fixed to the cord. If'n I'd a left her she'd a died. I couldn't do that. You know?"

"Yeah. I believe you. Rhonda's mama, Aileen, said the man that kept comin around was black-headed anyway. Yours is brown, mostly. You gotta little gray in there too. What you goin to do with her?"

"I don't even know Rhonda or her mama."

"No. Not Aileen. The baby. Susan. What you goin to do with her?"

"I'm goin to take care of her. For now."

"Then what?"

"You ast too damn many questions."

"Well, have you thought about it?"

Lige wanted to shriek like a girl. Pull his hair. Put his hands on his hips. He wanted to do all of those things because of course he'd thought about it and of course he had no idea what he was going to do later. He had a dim image in his mind of him and the baby and Danceray all together at some later point but right now he had to think about the present.

"Yeah. No. I only know I can't do it by myself."

"You want some help?"

"You offerin?"

"Yeah. I can help you with her. It ain't no problem."

"If'n I give you the money for the rest of them Pampers, can you bring em with you next time you come?"

"Sure."

"Another thing. I need to get enough supplies up here to make a batch a shine. But this time I need to triple the recipe, and peaches'll be ready in about a week. You know where I can get holt of a wagon?"

Ivy stared at Lige, with her eyes twinkling almost in laughter, for a few moments before she replied.

"What you need a wagon for? I got a four wheeler."

It was Lige's turn to stare.

"Well, I be damned. That's a good idea! But we can't leave Susan by herself up here to go get the stuff."

Lige glanced down at the ground in front of him, thinking.

"We ain't got to leave her up here by herself. You can go get all the stuff and I'll stay up here with her."

"I don't know if that's such a good idea or not."

Lige was nervous.

"I can take care of her. I got two little brothers and a baby sister."

"It ain't that. I trust you."

"What is it then?"

"I can't drive one a them things. I ain't even drove a truck or a car in years."

"You can do it. It's easy. I can teach you in five minutes. Maybe less."

"You sure about that?"

"Yep. I'm sure."

Lige carefully studied Ivy's face. He knew he was putting all his trust in this little rogue of a girl but he also knew that he had no other choice. Right now, he had Ivy or he had no one, and though he was unaccustomed to trust he pushed his doubts aside and took the plunge.

"Well, allrighty then. When you come tomorrow, bring them Pampers with you. And the four wheeler. Can't risk nobody seein us together just yet. You a have to do the teachin up here. There's a flat over yonder a ways. Susan can go with us in the basket."

"Okay. It's a plan."

Chapter 10

Lige stretched his back and twisted his neck, trying to crack stiff bones that had become tension-filled. After Ivy left the day before, he'd spent most of the evening drinking and digging. Susan slept almost the whole time. He never knew how much time babies spent sleeping. Seemed to him that's all Susan did. Sleep, eat, poop; sleep, eat, poop. Most people acted like babies were fun-filled little things that lifted the spirits and provided countless hours of story-telling. So far, there had been nothing she'd done that bore repeating. Even if her mama were still alive, Lige couldn't imagine any cute stories that she could come up with to tell her family or friends about Susan. Susan was boring. But Susan was becoming the most important person in his life. Susan had, in fact, become the reason he wanted to live. And though he couldn't imagine giving up the shine completely, even he knew that he drank a little less and kept a bit more conscious in order to listen to her while she slept. To listen for sounds of distress or discomfort—even if those sounds were so minuscule to be close to imperceptible.

In return for drinking less and sleeping lighter, Lige already suffered fewer headaches. His hands shook less forcibly in between stages of drunkenness. His eyes were less bleary and sensitive. There was less nausea and more hunger. Food tasted better and he believed nourished him more than in the past when it had to fight through the liquor-filled veins to accomplish clean absorption. He often was embarrassed about bathroom behaviors even in front of himself, and he certainly would never discuss such with others—even for medical reasons, unless the matter was of life and death—but he now had fewer bouts of diarrhea, more solid results. So much more so that he believed he might have to move the outhouse. Of course, the more he thought about that subject, that possibility, the more he questioned whether he was simply more aware. More sensitive to the odors and the outcomes. He felt his face burn with inner heat as he thought about it and glanced around knowing he was alone but feeling there were eyes watching him and knowing his thoughts, decided to leave it for another time.

But the digging had become almost as important to him as making this next, crucial batch of shine. With working steadily, even at Lige's age combined with the fact that he had become terribly out of shape over the last few years, he still was able to dig about eight feet down into the rich, loamy, mountain earth and four feet across. A couple times he'd become entangled with roots and vines that threatened to take his patience. He, however, prevailed until well after midnight at which point he sat down hard and finished off the bottle he had also been steadily working to conquer. When he had become too tired and too high to do much more physically, he took a scrap of paper and the carpenter's pencil. He wrote: cornmeal, sugar, yeast, malt. Lige didn't need to write down the quantities of the items he had to buy; he would just get each in the largest packaging he could find and buy as many as was necessary. He needed water too but that would come from the mountain. No need to buy it. These batches of moonshine had to be the largest enterprise of his career and he knew also that he would have to go out and solicit customers for it. The peach brandy would come next. He would also make blackberry brandy. Most folks liked the peach but some preferred blackberry and the blackberry ensured him more female buyers. Blackberry was also popular for medicines made at home. *Should I make some cough syrups while I'm at it?* Lige thought about the idea and quickly decided against it. Most women-folk would prefer their own recipes for remedies—he would just stick to what he did best. The shine.

He looked up into the sun and estimated the time to be around ten, ten-thirty at the latest, and wondered when Ivy would be there. He glanced over to where Susan lay sleeping and wondered when she would wake up to eat. He wasn't used to waiting on others for anything. Over the years, since Eller and the baby died, he had done just exactly what he wanted when he wanted and this feeling of allowing others to determine his activities was foreign and somewhat disconcerting to him. He was antsy, nervous. He couldn't start anything without either Ivy or Susan and he was unused to such dependent independency. In other words, he was in charge of everything, and therefore, independent, but could do nothing without one or both of them making the first move, and in that way he was dependent. Hell of a predicament to suddenly find himself in. On the other hand, these two people who'd so recently fallen into his sphere had become unbearingly important to him, and fast!

He found himself checking the path often wanting to see Ivy. Perhaps needing her company, perhaps simply needing anyone's company. And that was a need that he did not care to discuss at the moment, even with himself. Realizing that Susan was not ready to awaken and Ivy was not about to come out into the clearing from the path, he again lifted the shovel and began to pitch it into the earth at the bottom and around the sides of the hole, bringing up chunks of the world, throwing it to the sides over his shoulder and above his head. He had either read or heard somewhere, years ago, that if a person dug a hole all the way through the earth from anywhere in the United States that person would eventually end up in China. Was that the truth? If he kept digging would the first face he saw be a Chinaman? He laughed, thinking of the absurdity and the impossibility of actually doing such a thing. Lige stopped digging for a moment and wiped the sweat from his brow with the bandana he carried with him for sweat and nose-blowings.

"What the hell are you doing down there? Too deep for a grave."

Ivy. He hadn't heard her come up which meant she didn't have the four-wheeler. Disappointment washed over him because even though he was in some way afraid of learning to ride it, he needed to get those supplies up here on Pouter. He must, if his plans were going to work out, make this shine. And if he were to be honest, and it would be almost impossible for him to admit it to anyone else, he was also excited about learning to ride the four-wheeler. Careen used to say that no matter how old a man got he never grew up—always a little boy lived inside.

"I got to make a place down here to hide Susan in case anybody comes up here snoopin around."

Lige met Ivy's gaze, believing he could transfer the severity of the situation through the sheer effort of a look and silence, wanting to keep the worst from happening by not speaking it out loud, not speaking it into existence. Sometimes if you didn't give something a name, then that something was powerless against you. And right now, he would cling to any superstition, any hearsay, any claim, if it meant that the chances of keeping Susan safe were bettered. Ivy's face, however, became a mixture of disappointment and anger. At least Lige thought there was anger in her expression but he couldn't imagine a reason for anger. Disappointment either for that matter.

"What's a matter with you?"

"You think I told about the baby, don't you?"

"No. Did you?"

"Of course not! Why would I tell?"

"Don't know. Why wouldn't you?"

"Look man! I seen you take them Pampers. I come up here to see what was goin on and you told me about it all. I believed you. I believe you. I offered to help. I liked Rhonda. We won't best friends or nothin like that but she didn't deserve to die. I think it's sweet you tryin to take care of Susan. But if you want to be a son-of-a-bitch about it, then fine. Fuck off!"

Ivy turned toward the path.

"I didn't mean nothin by it. I'm just nervous that's all. You bring the four-wheeler?"

Ivy turned back to face him again.

"Yeah I brought it. Left it a ways down the path. There's a good place to ride over to the right of it. And I brought lunch."

Ivy sat down under the shelter and took four cheeseburgers and two orders of fries from the bag she brought with her. She patted the spot beside her, and motioned for him to come up out of the hole and sit beside her.

"Come on. Food's cold enough already. You better hurry up and eat anyway cause the baby's twistin around like she's goin to wake up soon. Welcome to motherhood!"

Lige kicked his boot into the dirt on the side of the hole, making a ledge to step up on and then made another so he was high enough up to step from the mouth of it. He brushed the dirt from his hands and then wiped them down the sides of his trousers in a gesture of hygiene before sitting beside Ivy.

"You're too young to know much about motherin. Where'd you learn so much?"

"My mama's had three babies after me, but I have to watch em a lot. Those two boys came ten months away from one another. Don't think I had two complete hot meals the first two years they was alive."

Lige laughed but the laughter did not come across as due to humor.

"Some folk have babies; some folk take care of em. Seems like to me anyway."

"You got that shit right. I wonder sometimes if she don't want to be a mama why she's always gettin preggo. There's ways around it these days."

"That's two good points there. Makes me wonder why you'd make the offer to help with Susan."

"Mama havin babies taught me a thing or two. One: I don't mind too much takin care of a baby here and there for a little while. Two: I don't want none of the little bastards for myself. Not for keeps anyway. And if you ain't goin to keep one why bother with makin it in the first place? Right?"

"Right. This here cheeseburger's good. I ain't had a cheeseburger in a long time."

Ivy looked over at her new friend and smiled. He had a clear grease streak running from his bottom lip into his beard. He smiled back and Susan began to cry.

"Make her bottle and I'll feed her. You need to finish eatin."

Lige liked her suggestion and readily agreed. He was tired of his own cooking which wasn't that good to begin with and there was just something about café food that once he started on it he couldn't resist keeping on. He came back in a few short minutes and handed the milk-glove to Ivy.

"What?"

"Huh? What, what?"

"Um, like what's this for?"

"It's her bottle."

"You got to be kiddin me!"

Lige watched her fingering the glove, squishing the milk around in the index finger tip.

"Seriously man?"

"Seriously. It's all I got."

Lige spread both arms out in front of him hands palms up.

"It's really a good idea, I guess. I'll bring a real bottle up here tomorrow though. Okay?"

"I should a thought about that yesterday when I ast you for the Pampers."

"No problem. I'll bring it tomorrow."

Ivy stood to get Susan from the sleeping mat. And when she began to feed her, Lige watched her face turn from a street-smart, edgy, young girl to that of an angelic, nurturing woman. She had, in the space of less than a minute, become The Mother. She instinctively cared for the child the way that in nature female animals care for their young with no previous instruction or knowledge of what to do or how to do it. They just do what needs to be done as if they'd done it as a matter of fact for the entirety of the lives they'd been given from the start. Was this kind of fostering care only possible in women? Could men find the same qualities from deep within their psyches? Or were they lacking some basic, fundamental trait? Could he do the same things for Susan? Be as good at it? Oh, he knew he was able to provide for the baby— give her all that she needs—but what he really wanted, needed, to know was whether he, a man, could take care of her. He closed his eyes offering a momentary prayer, that although was brief and to the point, he realized that his mind, body and soul had been repeating incessantly since the moment he laid eyes on Susan and the dead girl. He knew too that he should stop calling Susan's mama the dead girl. What if he thought of her as the dead girl so much and so often that when Susan asked him about her mother at some eventual, distant time, but not so distant to disallow the alarm for careful consideration, and pointed tact that he would blurt out that her mother, to him, was just the dead girl he found on the creek-bank. That would never do. Susan deserved much more and a good deal better than that from him. Even if he always thought of Rhonda as the dead girl, he must remember her name when Susan finally thought to ask where her mother was. And while he went about remembering her name there was nothing wrong, as far as he could see, with finding out all the information he could about Rhonda and any of her other family members as well. He knew that there were tons of folks looking for family to record by putting their names and when possible their faces on the branches of family trees. Family and everything about them as far back as one can recall or record was important. Family and their respective individual or collective nature and activity played an integral role in how one sees one's self and how one sees the world around the center of one's individuality. He didn't have to be a particularly intelligent man to understand that every single person in one's background helped to define and inform the present and on into the future of the structure of that unit. For no single person performing a single act can or will refrain from impact on the future generations of his or her kinsmen—the impact might be so subtle that it's almost unfelt or unknown, appearing as a whispered, unoriginated idea, or as a banging, crashing thought that stomps its way in and collides with and into every single neuron in the recipient's familial connection—never to be ignored and always to be valued.

But Lige was not a particularly intelligent man, neither was he one to dabble with profundity. Lige only knew that what was contained in his heart and enclosed in his mind were the only important matters for and to his past, present and into his future. Those stuffs would carry and support and promote him because of all of his family gone before him—his ancestors—and all of his kinfolk to come. And Susan, though not his flesh and blood, not linked to those from his past would flourish and grow and mature because of him and despite him and in this manner she would forever be a part of him and all that had ever been and that ever will be his family. Lige felt the chill of air on the sweat running the length of his spine—sweat that he had been unaware of until the moment that shared an edge with the thought that had come just before, just as, he thought one of the darkest, most forbidding of thoughts. What was it exactly that Danceray had said to him the night he stood before her in her house? What did she say about Tater? He promised himself that he would remember the exact words but again he had broken a promise. The thought and the statement were the very reasons he worked to dig the hole, the very reasons he knew that Susan was in danger, and the very reasons that he dreaded ever coming into contact with Tater again.

Of course, it was true that Tater held a grudge against him. Who would be unable to after what he did. Lige killed Tater's brother. Lige killed Rooster. Killing a person's brother was an act that no one forgave. No one ever forgot such a thing. No one said, *Oh, you killed my*

brother but I ain't mad at you. It's okay. No problem.
Because even if a person's brother deserved the killing, the remaining family members believed the murder was uncalled for. Sure, Danceray had said she wasn't mad at him for killing her husband. She was, however, only mad at him for taking away her chance at being a mother. Danceray was not related by blood to Rooster. Marriage didn't guarantee a loyalty that blood did. But now, though he hadn't in fact forgotten what Danceray had said, he just hadn't allowed the comment to reach down into the depth of his comprehension. For to comprehend what Danceray had actually meant by what she'd said, required him to dig the metaphorical hole to the other side of the world—to look a Chinaman in the face. And in the exact moment, the comprehension came as easily as scraping a scab off the surface of the skin. *Tater's some way involved in this; I just ain't figured out how yet.* True, those may not be her words verbatim but they were close. If Tater was involved in the situation the only way in which he would be involved was if he either murdered the girl or was with the person who did. And why murder a pregnant girl? Who commits that kind of atrocity?

"Ivy? You said an older man was involved with that girl? Rhonda?"

Ivy held Susan up half thrown across her shoulder and patted her back roughly and rhythmically. Lige thought the patting was a bit too rough but he didn't say so. Instead, he watched her face and waited for the answer he so desperately needed from her.

"Yeah. Her mama said so."

"Do you know what he looked like?"

97

"Not really. Aileen said he had black hair. And she said he had a black heart. That's all I heard. Why?"

"I don't know. I can't be sure but I might know who he is."

Lige dropped his napkin onto the paper bag that lay between them. There was some tomato pulp with four or five seeds hanging onto the red flesh of the tomato middle laying there in a puddle of mayonnaise.

"Who?"

"For right now it's better for you not to know. Just steer clear of men around my age."

"What about you? I need to steer clear a you too?"

Lige looked closely at her. He'd been living alone so long that he no longer had devices with which to measure others. He believed she was joking but knew even if she was there was nothing funny about any of what was going on. If Tater killed Rhonda, anyone who came close to her either now or in the past would be in danger.

"No. But if you're scared a me, then you better go now. If you're just pickin, then you better go ahead and teach me about that four-wheeler."

Susan burped, sounding like a man in a bar after having too many beers too close together.

"You want to pack her up how ever way you was plannin to so we can head out?"

Chapter 11

The same morning that Lige made his way back down
Salter Ridge with Susan and the supplies and directions
that Danceray had given him, Tater, Eustus Jr. and Blacky
made their way back up the ridge. And in fact, it was only
by the grace of God that they had not crossed paths at any
of three different junctures. Perhaps if Lige had lingered
over a third cup of coffee or if Eustus Jr. hadn't gone off
into the woods and stayed for seven or eight minutes then
they might have come face to face during their separate
journeys. It was only after Eustus Jr. had stepped off into
the woods for the second time, however, that Blacky made
a somewhat dim connection. The first time, he'd thought
Eustus Jr. was attending the call of nature but when he
went the second time he realized that while it was
possible he needed to relieve himself again or in a
different way it was not probable. Both Tater and Eustus
Jr. carried packs that they wore across one shoulder and
with the straps over their heads much the same way that
Frenchmen carried bags that looked like pocketbooks or
purses. Blacky knew that neither man would carry such a
feminine item as a purse. The front of the packs were
flapped over and clinched with a metal twist clasp. And
though he knew that most people would believe that the
fact that Eustus Jr. came out of the woods the second time
with the pack on the opposite side of his body from when
he'd gone in was of little or no importance, he'd learned
over the years that the truth was always in the details. If a
person paid attention to all of the details not just the big
picture that person would always be ahead of the game,
whatever the game was. Blacky was gifted with the knack

for noticing and keeping track of every, single, solitary detail and the knowledge that what may seem unimportant in one moment when the worm turned into the next that piece of information became all that mattered, all that meant anything. In fact, though he couldn't explain how it happened, he would bet on his mother's life that the smallest detail was what solved all riddles. And in this way, the very thing that made him a good criminal had the same potential to make him a good criminalist. Maybe one day, he too would cross the line, switch the metaphorical pack to the opposite side— become an officer of the law. So, because the pack was on the other shoulder crossing his head in the other direction, he could assume that Eustus Jr. had taken the pack off, if even for a moment, and then replaced it as if it was a mirror image of itself.

He glanced over at Tater's pack and saw that it was on the same shoulder he'd carried it on since they'd come up on top of Pinter Mountain. And not only that, but also Tater's pack hung limply, empty from his shoulder swinging aimlessly with no weight. The pack Eustus Jr. carried, on the other hand, hung densely, bulging from unidentified contents. Would they tell him if he asked what the packs were for? Seemed to him that the two of them wanted to keep the packs' purpose a secret. Otherwise, wouldn't one or both of them have commented on their use before now? Maybe he could get some information about them out of Miranda. He was better with women; they liked him. Men didn't often trust him and if he told the truth then he'd say they were better off not to. Women did trust him and he was careful to give them something for their trust. When he was with a woman, whether he loved her not, he made her feel that she was the only human being on earth who meant anything to him. And in those moments, she was. He didn't go so far as to lie to them. They were important and he loved loving them. He never told them they were the only one, or that the two of them would be together forever. Anything even remotely like that, any hopes or expectations were made up entirely in their own minds. And though he had been conscious of the fact, even though he had not consciously thought of the reality, almost every woman he'd ever made love with would shelter him, feed him, clothe him and in fact, help in any he needed if he asked. All he had to do was ask. He was happy to leave bridges unburned, to leave channels opened and to be able to step in the same tracks he'd earlier made.

He would find out from Miranda what those packs contained. She would tell him and not even realize that she'd given him anything he desired. Of course, Miranda was not a stupid girl; she was, as far as he could tell, smarter than the rest of her family. Perhaps even shrewd. But he was adept at obtaining information while asking questions that seemed so innocent, so innocuous, that others allowed the words to fall from their lips like water through a net. He had never used the word charming to refer to himself but that was what he was. Charming. These were the thoughts he contemplated and enjoyed as he followed behind the other two men on the paths working their way along the trails back to Salter Ridge, not knowing where he was going, unable to take the lead and content to tag along. When they came to the fork on Salter where a choice must be made to go to the left or right, he knew they should turn to the left but Tater veered to the right, and while he wondered why, he didn't ask. He simply walked in behind and figured he would know the reason in due time. Still, he did not trust Tater. He did not like him and if he were honest he would admit that he was disgusted by his evil nature and maybe even a little afraid of it and him. Tater was, he thought, like a rabbit. You think he's going one way and he goes the other with no warning. Just a shot and jab and he's gone.

Without meaning to think on it, the day Tater killed the pregnant girl came to his mind. He didn't need the images to come into his mind, take a seat and get comfortable. He couldn't look them in the eye as they lounged around wanting attention that he couldn't give. Needing assurance that everything would be all right if they just trusted and believed in the good, in the God, and in mankind. Those images, the dead girl, Tater coming out of the dump as if nothing of consequence had occurred. It was all too much for a man like him. His background, though colorful and peppered with incidences was a small, pale comparison to someone like Tater Shifflett. Tater didn't value the lives or the sensibilities of others. Blacky pushed the images to the back of his mind just as forcefully as he would if he were to throw people out of his house and lock the door behind them but those images were replaced with another one from the past few days. These images involved Tater's grandbaby, Tater's oldest daughter, Lilly's boy, Herschel. They all called him Hersh. He was a friendly child most of the time. Outgoing and rambunctious. Blacky liked him. Blacky liked most kids; they were honest even when they weren't supposed to be. He liked that. He could respect that and thought the world might be better if grown-ups would play by the same rules. One thing he'd noticed about Hersh though was that he didn't like Tater and that dislike was the main quality

102

about Hersh that Blacky could admire. The boy was beyond his years in that sentiment, maybe—maybe kids knew first and best. On the particular day that was now in question, now in review, in Blacky's mind, Blacky had walked into the house directly behind Tater and the same distance in front of Eustus Jr. and Hersh was playing on the floor in the middle of the front room. He had some kind of wooden toy. Seemed like it might have been a homemade choo-choo train or some such as that. Blacky watched Tater smiling as he headed straight to the spot where Hersh sat and for a moment Blacky thought he witnessed a tender moment between Tater and his grandson. Hersh looked up when the shadow of Tater's body fell over the area surrounding him.

"What you doin boy?"

Still Tater smiled, sweetly, the emotion so foreign to his face that it contorted into wickedness.

"Playin."

Hersh smiled up at Tater.

"Playin? Pussies play. You a pussy, boy?"

"No."

"No? You back-talkin me?"

"No."

It happened so quickly that Blacky didn't even see it coming. Tater reached out and slapped Hershel across the face sending him sprawling, holding his stinging cheek. Blacky saw the red marks of a handprint but the boy did not cry. Instead, he looked at his grandpa showing a sense of gratitude that he had not confused him with a kindness he had never before experienced or expected from him.

Now, Blacky followed Tater up the trail, which alternately widened and narrowed and twisted and turned until finally it opened out into a tidy yard in front of a well-kept, small house. Tater stepped up on the porch, strode to the door and without knocking opened it and walked right in. Blacky followed and Eustus Jr. brought up the rear. The sun was barely up and here the three of them were waltzing into someone's house. He hoped they were welcome in this house; he didn't want trouble. Didn't need it and didn't court it.

"Danceray! You up?"

Momentarily, Blacky heard movement from the back of the house and then a small, dark-haired woman came from the darkness out into the open front room. She wore a mint green house-robe over her white gown, he knew because he saw the collar and hemline, even though she held the top of the gown closed with a hand small enough to be a child's. There must be a man around here somewhere because she wore a thin gold band on the third finger of the hand holding the bodice. Whoever he was, wherever he was, from the looks of that wedding band, if one could weigh love from the weight of gold, she was one more unloved woman.

"I am now. What's goin on?"

"That's a fine welcome. Make us some breakfast."

Blacky couldn't lie; he was starving but he thought Tater was way out of line with the way he spoke to her, whoever she was. Of course, there was no introduction. Tater sat down at the table.

"Eustus Jr. stoke up the fire."

"What you want to eat?"

"Whatever you got's fine. Maybe some fried eggs, bacon, ham, gravy. Biscuits too."

Tater glanced at the coffee pot.

"Got coffee?"

"No, Tater. Not made anyway. I don't usually make it in my sleep."

"Ha-ha. You a funny woman now, huh?"

Tater slapped her on the ass when she turned toward the coffee pot and she jumped but Blacky didn't think it was for pleasure.

"Aunt Danceray? You got any of that persimmon jelly you make?"

Aha! She was Eustus Jr.'s aunt so that meant she was either Tater's sister or sister-in-law. Now it was all making a little more sense.

"Yeah. Ain't got none open though. Go out on the back porch and look on the top shelf. In behind the strawberry preserves should be some."

"You don't care?"

"You don't care?" Tater mimicked.

Eustus Jr. turned to look his father in the eye and for the first time Blacky noticed real animosity in the young man for his father. Does Tater even know how his son feels about him? He doubted it. And that was the exact moment he knew Tater's weakness. He had no perception. He operated at the base, gut level and anybody who did that would not win in the end. People like him never did. They lost and they lost in the most horrible of ways. People like Tater never saw the final blow come. That was where even little Hershel had Tater beat. Hershel always saw the blow coming and he would prevail in the future because of the ability to trust what he distrusted. Tater, on the other hand, could only be a bully. He got what he wanted by browbeating, harassing, intimidating and otherwise terrorizing others. But he wouldn't, couldn't, maintain that advantage because it was impossible to never miss a step, to never underestimate. Blacky relaxed into this revelation. He was no longer afraid of Tater Shifflett. The sun didn't shine up one dog's ass all the time and that was a plain fact. Tater's day was coming. And that day would be a dark day for him, full of shock and awe. Blacky hoped he would be there to see it, to watch the chips fall. Danceray asked Blacky for the second time how he liked his eggs before he realized that she'd spoken to him.

"Oh. Any way you make em's fine with me. I can eat eggs any way cept raw."

Tater didn't say anything but when Blacky glanced over at him he saw loathing in his eyes. He hated Tater's ungiving, unforgiving eyes and for a brief moment thought he would gain tremendous pleasure in poking them out and once again he wondered what in the Devil's hell he was doing here with this passionately wild circle of

106

mountain people. True, most of them were delightful in an unfamiliar and unusual way but he could easily believe that he'd been dropped from a space ship onto the strange, foreign terrain around these alien people who once you think you understand something about them they shift on you. Mercurial in nature; quicksilver in action.

"Danceray? You seen any strangers up around here anywhere?"

"What you mean strangers?"

She set out coffee cups, milk and sugar and then brought the coffee pot to set in the middle of the table on a trivet.

"Help yourselves with that. Ya'll want grits too?"

"Be good. Strangers. You know like in people we don't know."

"No. Ain't been nobody around here. I don't know about down your road. Ain't talked to none a your people since you been gone."

"Dance, now listen to me. This here's important. You'd tell me if somebody'd been here, right?"

Blacky watched her face. Her pupils tightened up and the right side of her upper lip twitched once. Just once in the upward direction and stayed there until after she replied. *Damn! He's stupid. And the worst part is he thinks he's smart. He's dangerous.*

"Yeah. Sure. I'd tell you. What's the use in lyin?"

"That's right, right there! No use in lyin. You know I'd find out sooner or later anyway."

That's not what she means you idiot fuck! Eustus Jr. poured some coffee out onto his saucer and drank from the rim of it. Danceray set the breakfast plates out in front of them and then brought the bread warmer to the table. Blacky watched Eustus Jr. lift the lid off the bread warmer, take a biscuit from inside and then dunk it in his coffee cup.

"What the hell you doin man?"

"Soaky bread! You ain't never had none?"

Blacky shook his head not sure about anything called soaky bread. Strange people, strange food, strange everything. Florida, oh Florida, how I love and miss you. Once I get my feet back down on your flat, expansive ground, I might never leave you again. He thought about seeing people on television kissing the ground upon their return to America. He just might do that same thing once he crossed the state-line. But for now he'd bide his time, let this trip play itself out, and what the hell? He would try soaky bread. He took a biscuit and dipped it in the coffee.

"Hey now! That's pretty good."

Eustus Jr. spurred on by Blacky's approval nodded his head up and down.

"If'n you like this I tell you what to try. Cornbread and milk. You can crumble it up in sweet milk but buttermilk's better. You can do it with a biscuit too but cornbread's the way to go!"

Once again, Tater mimicked his son but this time he didn't use words. Instead, he hummed a tune to the words Eustus Jr. had just left in the air between them.

"Why you always got to be so fuckin mean, anyway? Can't you just be agreeable sometimes? Would it fuckin kill you?"

"There you go, Jr. Stand up for yourself for once. Be a man. Damn sure didn't know you had it in you!"

"I'm a man! I'm a man. You just don't know how much a man I am yet!"

"Naw boy. Tell you what's the truth. Didn't know you had any manliness in you. Proud of you, is what I am. Now shut the hell up fore I knock the shit out of you."

Blacky wanted to laugh and he wanted to say something to Tater but knew he needed to just sit quietly. He toyed around with the insight into Tater's character like a cat with a still, live-warm mouse. The time would come. Just wait it out. And what the hell? If he went back to Florida before Tater got his comeuppance, he could go with the knowledge that the day would come; it had to. There was no other way where his kind was concerned.

Chapter 12

Lige had to admit that the past week had been among the most fun-filled of his life. Ivy, true to her word, taught him to ride the four wheeler, he built a structure that was part litter, part wagon to pull behind it, he finished digging the underground room to hide Susan in if she was in danger, and he hauled in three trips up Pouter Mountain from Mabry's Crossing enough supplies to make the shine. He'd brought up sugar in a fifty pound bag, twenty-five pounds of cornmeal, a canister of yeast, a canister of malt, and he bought a larger container to hold the mash while he prepared it for distilling. He had done a great deal of work and there was still more to do. The peaches would be ready next week. The rain had held off causing them to be a week later than expected but there was no use getting them until they were ready. He'd get the peaches, raisons and lemons at the same time and then he'd make the peach brandy. Ivy had turned into the biggest asset of his life. Whatever he needed, her hands were right there beside him to turn the deed. Sometimes he didn't even have to vocalize the need before she was fulfilling it. Ivy was such a capable person that any task became manageable. She was the right hand to his left. If he made plans from his dreams, she calculated the manner to bring them to fruition, and by the same token if he made measurements or premeditated a shell of a design then she figured out how to fill it in. No matter from which angle he came, Ivy saw into it and commenced from the opposite approach and in this way there was nothing at which they would fail. She was like the twin to his mind, the mirror to his thoughts. If he were a structure, then she was his engine. When he first realized that they worked together the way they did, he was almost embarrassed because he had not in the beginning understood the way he felt about her. Ivy was half his age. Ivy, to him, was a child. But he couldn't deny that his feelings for her went beyond the surface; his feelings for her were in no way superficial. In fact, where Ivy was concerned, his heart was too small a container. Sometimes just thinking of her caused him to be overcome with emotion. One night, after Susan was fed and diapered and content in the depths of sleep, Lige thought about the ways in which his life had changed in a matter of days and he was thankful—more than thankful. He experienced a sense of gratitude that physically slammed him face down on the ground. He cried the weeping of the most humble and most blessed. And he didn't understand a smidgen of what he felt. When he was emptied and drained of everything that was within him, he felt the vibrations of the earth again filling him, renewing him, and rejuvenating him until he believed he might explode. He carefully and warily brought himself to a sitting position—watching the boundaries of his encampment. He knew, without admitting, what he watched for. He sought the demons at the edges but they were no longer there. He took a long drink from his bottle and sat back against the nightstand listening to Susan's heavy breathing in the darkness. The demons were gone and Ivy and Susan were here in their places. And then he knew exactly what it was that he felt for and about Ivy. She, too, was his daughter. Ivy and Susan. And if he never had any other person, even Danceray, in his life he knew he would be fine. He could now, finally and irrevocably, allow Eller and the baby to rest in peace. Lige knew now that even though they were no longer with him, no longer on earth, no longer among the quick that they were still, albeit in some other form, right there near him and at the same time at the other end of the universe. And he was all right. He was all right.

Once again he thought about family and what it meant to be a member of a family. One certainly chose his friends but didn't they, couldn't they, also choose their family? Hadn't he made that choice with Susan the day he cut her loose from her mama and scrambled away with her? The night he'd scurried down Pouter and up Salter? From the moment he walked out of that dump carrying her and the ashtray, he claimed her. Otherwise, wouldn't he have taken her to the authorities? Sure, he told himself he didn't want to do that because there was the strong probability that they would try and pin Rhonda's murder on him. But even then, he knew there would be no evidence against him. And hadn't he chosen Ivy after she confronted him with the theft of a handful of Pampers, when he decided to trust her, to bring her into the circle of his life. And further, hadn't Ivy chosen him somehow and for some reason when she came up on Pouter in the first place? There had been a reason for all of these connections that none of them had understood at the outset but either understood now or would come to understand at some point. They had each chosen the others. Of course, he knew that one could easily argue that Susan had chosen no one but would that argument be correct? Hadn't she been the one to cry out? Might her soul, the part of her that was ancient compared to the tiny body it occupied, have cried out to him, knowing that he was her one chance to live, to survive and to eventually thrive? Yes, that is exactly what happened. And then when he had prayed that first night and Eller spoke to him, telling him to go to Danceray, Eller had been a part of those choices. What if? Wait. What if Susan's soul was the same soul that tried to live in his own little baby's body? It could be true. Maybe that was why Eller got involved in the first place. Or maybe Eller just missed Lige and wanted to help. Maybe he needed to stop thinking these thoughts but even as he tried to chase them from his mind a feeling of belonging settled upon him and for the first time in many years he knew for certain and true they would all be all right as long as they had each other.

Lige became aware of the noise gradually. The noise came over him like when something from the real world interfered with a dream, incorporating itself into the dream like that one time when the alarm clock had become a bird chirping fiercely, frantically at him. By the time he recognized the noise as something on the outside rather than the inside of his brain the noise was almost upon him. He had to be more careful than this! He anxiously took in everything around him. Could he get Susan down into the underground room quickly enough to keep her from danger? He struggled to his feet not knowing if he was weak from emotion or old age. He was only forty-two but those forty-two years had been lived hard. He hurried to the baby and scooped her up and then moved to make his way to the trap-door in the ground, the only thought in his mind was Susan's safety. Just as he closed his hand around the handle of the door, he heard the voice from about ten feet away.

"Elijah?"

The voice was one that he would recognize above all others, even his own. In fact, though the possibility might not seem real, he knew the source of the voice just at the moment she took in the breath before speech. The voice belonged to Danceray and for an amount of time that Lige had no way of measuring he could not breathe, he could not move, he could not function in any way. Danceray always, always had this effect on him. One moment, he was his normal self, and one word from her and he was both and neither himself. How did one person cause such a reaction in another? When would it end? And even worse was the question of how he would be himself if the feeling ever did go away. How would there be a Lige Worley if that person no longer loved Danceray Woodruff. Of course he knew her name hadn't been Woodruff in over twenty years but in his mind she would always be Danceray Woodruff unless and until she became Danceray Worley. Finally, he turned to face her.

"Danceray. You come here by yourself?"

"Of course, I come by myself."

"Nobody followin you?"

"Nope. Made sure of it. Doubled back twice. Took me forever to get here because of it too."

"Well then, I'm real glad to see you. You hungry? I got some popcorn."

"I ate. But I brought you some pork chops and a pone a bread. Thought you might be wantin some home cookin. Don't reckon you ever got too good at it yourself."

"I had some pork beans earlier but what you got sure sounds good. You want some coffee?"

"That'd be nice. And maybe some of the other too."

Lige knew she meant she'd have a drink or two of the shine but she wouldn't just come out and say it. That was fine. She was a lady and ladies didn't just come out and say indelicate statements. Lige stoked the fire in the pit, moving the embers, which were already dying down for the night, and ignited new sparks of life. He set the grill-rack back over the top of the fire and then went to the tree to pull down the coffee and sugar bags. He didn't use cream in his coffee but he reckoned if Danceray wanted some then he could just use some of the powdered milk he still kept from when he'd relied on it to feed Susan. Ivy had brought some real baby formula from the Dollar General when she brought the bottle. She said they had Similac and Enfamil but she thought the Enfamil was better so she chose it. Actually, there had not been a day that went by that Ivy hadn't brought at least one new item for Susan and lunch for Lige. And he had certainly not complained. He loved the greasy cheeseburgers, grilled cheeses, hot dogs all the way, chicken sandwiches, barbeques and the fat, crinkle-cut fries. And ranch dressing. Before now he'd always used Thousand Island whenever there was a call for any dressing. But since Ivy had shown him how to dip his fries in the creamy, white stuff he loved it so much that he poured it over practically everything he ate. He couldn't think of much that it didn't improve. He was grateful to and for Ivy Benton for many reasons but the fact that she anticipated needs and filled them made her indispensable just on that one level. To say the least, he'd almost stopped pulling down most of the bags he kept fastened high in the tree and relied on Ivy to bring him on a daily basis whatever she thought was the best choices in foods and drinks. Except for the shine and that was one thing he would probably never give up and ranch dressing couldn't improve upon.

He brought the coffee to the fire and measured it out into the basket of the pot. He noticed his hands were shaking and wondered if Danceray did too.

"Here, Lige, let me finish the coffee. You go get the other stuff."

Danceray took the task from him and he went to the shelter, checked on the sleeping baby and retrieved the bottle. When he held it up to the light he saw that it was only missing a finger or so. Good. He didn't know how much Danceray wanted to drink but at least he had it right here for her. If she wanted more than what was in this bottle, then he'd go down into the underground room and pull another one. He wondered if he should show her the huge emerald cluster he'd unearthed while digging. That cluster was at least as big around as his head, maybe larger—he wouldn't know until he pulled the whole thing out, like extracting a giant molar—but one thing he did know was that that one gemstone would earn him enough money to live for the rest of his life and a few other people's lives too. Tater and Eustus Jr. could go all around the mountains hunting ginseng all they wanted, but Lige knew after the emerald, Pouter Mountain would also provide rubies, garnets, amethyst, topaz, tourmaline and God only knows what else. All he had to do was to dig. So far, Ivy was the only other person who knew. He would wait. Fools rush in, and he didn't want to be a fool. Not again. First, he needed to know what brought her to Pouter Mountain this late at night. True, the evening was fabulously gorgeous. The sky was clear and bright even in darkness, the stars a jeweled mantle hovering low and dense. He felt as if he could reach up to the heights and gently pull the blanket over their bodies as they sat high on Pouter listening to the serenade of the night-singing

116

crickets and croaking bull-frogs. With every strident chirp and each discordant throaty grumble, Lige felt the vibration deep in the seat of his person. He believed that there was a vibration from overhead, from the night-sky and from all around and under the ground energizing him, his body, his soul. But the truth of the matter, and he knew this more and better than anything else he knew, was that Danceray was the vibration pulsating into and through him physically, spiritually and mentally. Danceray made him ultra-alive. He thought now about how indifferent he'd been over the years since Danceray married Rooster, and then even more so after Eller and the baby died. When they died, if the truth was told, Lige went a little crazy, knowing there was not one single person left on the earth that belonged to him or he belonged to. He recalled now, for the first time in ages, how he'd gathered a few personal items from the house and set them down on the middle of the yard. He then walked into the shed, grabbed the gas can and marched straight back into the house. He poured gas over their furniture, rugs and beds. He slung it onto and across the walls. Still, to his way of thinking, there was not enough gas, so he went back to the shed. True, at the time he was insane, wild with madness, up the pole with pain-induced agitation. Once back in the shed, he found no more gas, no more fuel to add to the dousing, so he grabbed the handle of the lawnmower and rolled it easily up to the front porch and then pulled it backward up the steps. He was strong—stronger than he'd ever been. He lifted the lawnmower and flung it through the front door, uncapped the gas tank and left the machine on its side. Standing in the middle of the room, feeling his feet sink spongily the depth of maybe an eighth of an inch into the gas-soaked rug, and not caring if he lived or died—for to die was too easy and to live too difficult—he struck the match and pitched it toward one corner of the room, struck another and chucked it in the other direction. He had not left the room immediately; instead, he stood watching the flames rise from the floor, billowing, and swelling up and up toward the ceiling. The flames mesmerized him and he almost stood too long inside the manufactured hell. He wanted every single speck and smidgen of the life he'd made with Eller to disappear. The life that although was not full of passion and arduous excitement was bursting with easiness, contentment and sweet companionship.

Now, with Danceray sitting by the fire close enough for him to reach out and touch her, he shook his head to clear it of thoughts of Eller and the baby and the fire, and even the loneliness of the years that came after. There was a difference, a vast difference, between loneliness and solitude. Until recently, he had been lonely, now he enjoyed the moments of solitude. The times when he was secluded comfortably on Pouter Mountain between Ivy's last visit and her next, between Susan's last nap and her next, were some of the most satisfying of his life. During these times, he knew for the first time he could only go forward, things could only get better. Lige handed Danceray a small, juice glass and a coffee cup and took a seat beside her. She picked up the coffee pot, filled both their cups and then held her cup out to him to add liquor to it. He poured a healthy amount into her black coffee and then laughed when she held out the juice glass too and he filled it half full.

"Why'd you come up here?"

"You ain't never been about beatin around the bush, have you?"

"Ain't much need for it."

"You mind me bein here?"

"No, I mind when you ain't."

"You don't beat around the bush and you tell the truth. Fatal flaws or life-affirmin merits?"

"I don't have no way to judge it but I don't have no way to change it neither."

"I reckon I'll be honest too then. I come up here to see you."

Lige reached out and patted her knee, his large hand covering her petite knee-cap. He wanted to leave his hand where it lay but did not want to risk being offensive.

"I'm happy you did."

"How's the baby?"

"She's doin real fine. Real fine."

"I'm proud a you, Elijah."

"Ain't no need for pride. Anybody'd do the same thing."

Danceray watched his face measuring her next words carefully.

"No. You're wrong. Not many people would."

This time, she reached out and patted his knee, her tiny hand barely perceptible in weight but even so, scorched its way through his skin, his muscle, his bone and all the way to the back of his brain. Her touch was almost unbearable to him. He wanted her to touch him unendingly. He needed her to cover him. He thought of the song called *Cover Me* and though he'd never made a connection to it in the past, he now understood the lyrics on a level deep in his soul almost completely untapped, untouched. Her touch brought to the surface every scrap of love he contained.

"Lige. There's another reason I'm here too."

"Do tell."

"Tater came by the house after you left with the baby. Like to a scared me to death. Eustus Jr. was with him and some black guy. Name's Blacky Johnson—no, Jackson. Tater ast me questions about if anybody'd been up on Salter, any strangers."

"Yeah. That night I was there you said Tater was involved with the dead girl—Rhonda—and Susan but you didn't know how yet. You think he killed her?"

"I think so. If he didn't kill that girl he was with whoever did. Or he wouldn't be worried about anybody comin up on the mountain. That Blacky guy might've done it too. He's real quiet. Just sat around watchin and listenin. Seems like a smart feller. Too smart for Tater anyway. And Tater don't like that none too much."

"Most everybody's too smart for Tater. Is that all he wanted to know? Who's been on the mountain?"

"Yeah. That's all he ast about. Demanded breakfast."

Danceray handed her juice glass to him. He refilled the glass, took two large swallows from the bottle and screwed the cap back on. He didn't want to get too drunk with Danceray here. He would want to be aware of everything that happened and everything she said. He wouldn't want to miss a thing.

"Well, thanks for lettin me know."

"I'm worried he's goin to put it all together somehow. Figure it out."

"If he does we'll deal with it then."

"But what about Susan? How can you protect her up here all by yourself? And I can't take her over on Salter with me. All it would take would be for Tater to know I had her and it would all be over. Even if he don't want her himself, he'd know we knew something about her mama's killin."

"Susan's safe here. Come here and let me show you something."

Lige stood to his feet, picked up the lantern from beside where he'd sat and reached down to take her hand—to help her up from the ground. Once she was standing, she took a minute to get her legs under her good and then nodded that she was ready. He walked over to the trap-door, kicked the brush and dirt from the top and pulled the door up with the handle, motioning for her to follow. Danceray cautiously stepped onto a wooden step and then just where she expected the next step to be, stepped down onto another and then another. After the third step, she stepped down onto the soft earth and glanced around at the dirt-packed walls. Her eyes adjusted to the semi-darkness that was even darker than the semi-darkness of above ground. There were no stars down where they stood now. Nothing but the lantern. Being there with another man might have frightened her but not with Lige. Lige, of all people, made her feel safe but she was curious and confused.

"What's all this?"

"It's a safe-house. For Susan. Hell, I guess for me too. And Ivy. In case somebody comes up here and we have to hide."

Lige looked deeply into Danceray's eyes and saw fear and worry.

"Oh Lige! He'll come up here. I just know he will. He's not the smartest man but he don't give up. He don't!"

Lige opened his mouth to speak but she took a step closer to him and stopped his words.

"Who the hell's Ivy?"

Lige's heart thumped. Was she jealous? She was. She was jealous. He might have been living up here alone all these years but he knew a jealous bone when he come up on one.

"Ivy?"

He decided to play with her for a minute or two—as long as she'd allow it anyway.

"Yes, Ivy."

"What do you know about Ivy?"

"Just what you just now said. In case somebody comes up here and y'all have to hide. You said Ivy."

Lige knew he should let it go—tell her about Ivy—but he had to admit that he was enjoying her jealousy which had begun to flirt with anger. He hadn't had any woman show him any amount of caring in such a long time that now for Danceray to express even the slightest shred of jealousy made him react like a teenager—the teenager who'd watched her marry another man while his own despair-filled heart split open, and ruined, fell to pieces.

"Oh. Ivy? She's a friend of mine. Comes up here about every day to help out. She helped make this room, helps with Susan, hell, pardon my language, she even taught me to ride a four-wheeler. Helps me make the shine. She's a good girl."

"Well! Fine then. I see I shouldn't be a worryin about you!"

Danceray scrambled back up the steps she'd just descended, trusting him perhaps with her life for she didn't know for certain what kind of man he'd become over the years. He could just as easily be the murderer of that young girl. People went crazy and never thought to tell another person about it. Crazy people didn't think they were crazy, did they? She was halfway across the clearing before Lige caught up to her.

"Ivy's twenty-two or three, I guess. She's just a young girl. I met her at the Dollar General. She works in there. Truth told, she saw me steal some Pampers for the baby that mornin after I come down from your house. I could a paid for em but that would've risked people knowin about Susan and I couldn't do that. Crazy thing followed me up here and confronted me. She didn't know if I killed the girl or not. Ever since that day we been together as friends. And I couldn't think more of her more if'n she was my own kid."

Danceray lifted her head, chin out, eyebrows high.

"You couldn't a said that before?"

"I'm sorry Danceray. Really. I was just havin fun."

Lige watched her expression soften from anger to relief.

"That was real dangerous business her comin up here like that. Don't she have a mama teachin her nothin?"

"She's got a mama but I don't think I think much of her. Not from the stories I hear anyway. Thinks more of herself than her kids."

Lige could no longer refrain from doing what he wanted to do more than anything in the world. He reached out and gently, softly ran that backs of the fingers of his right hand down her face, barely touching the skin of her cheek, while her cheek touched the skin of his fingers in such a way that he would never forget the feel of it. She leaned into his touch and though he knew he ran the risk of alienating her from him for the rest of his life he also knew that the love he felt for her either had to finally have its way or he would have to find a means to be rid of it. He could no longer live in this indeterminate state of always loving and yearning for the love to be returned to him.

124

Always unrequited. But even more than this was the constant nagging question: what went wrong, what went wrong, what went wrong... he did not, could not, know the answer but finally he would ask the question aloud. He would court the answers and either be reunited, vindicated or crushed, flattened from them or by them.

"Danceray?"

"Um-hmm?"

"What happened?"

Lige did not have to repeat the question or clarify it. Danceray didn't turn the question around or pull it apart; she didn't make him squirm, nor did she cause him to lose respect for himself by begging her. She simply answered the question he asked.

"Rooster told me he would kill you if I didn't marry him. When I told him you won't afraid of him he said he'd kill Eller."

"Eller loved him."

"I know. I lost a good friend doin what I did marryin him. But I believed he meant what he said. It won't till later, when it was too late, I knew he was full of shit."

"I always thought if Rooster and Eller was married she'd a been a match for him. He wouldn't a been able to hurt her the way he done you."

"He could only hurt her heart not her body. She'd a fought him. And he could hurt my body but not my heart. That's the difference."

Lige thought about what she said and when the full meaning of her words sunk in he thought he'd never heard such profundity. He had never been one to mince words; he didn't know how.

"Did you love me, Danceray?

"Yes. Very much. Did you love me, Elijah?"

"I loved you then and I love you still. That never changed. Never stopped."

"What about Eller? Did you love her too?"

"I loved Eller. The love was different than the love I kept for you. Eller never stopped lovin Rooster right up till the day she died. I guess when I killed him I ruined more than one life. After Rooster was dead though Eller had no hope for a turned future. She knew nothin, no matter what, would ever bring him back to her. Before, when he was still livin, Eller could hope just the way I hoped to have you back one day, some day. Hope's a wicked winged thing. Brings more hurt and harm than anything else."

"I always thought about us—you and me—gettin back together. But for one thing, I won't sure how you felt about me after what I done. For another, how could I rightly interfere with you and Eller just because Rooster was dead and me free? What would that a left Eller with? And that's assumin you would've still loved me. You know?"

Lige nodded his head. He did know. There had been many times after Rooster died, after he killed him with the axe, that Lige had thought about heading straight up Salter Ridge and to her door. He thought about taking

126

her into his arms, telling her how much he loved her, how he'd always loved her and always would, picturing in his mind the various outcomes of those actions. But the guilt he felt for taking Rooster's life—well, not so much for the killing but for those who were left in its wake—always prevailed, prevented him from having his heart's desire. It was true that even Eller understood what he done in killing Rooster. She knew that Lige had acted in the only way a man who knew that the woman he loved more than anything in the world suffered at the mercy of and under the brutality of another man's hands. Eller, of all people, understood vengeance.

"Yeah, I do know. What do we do now?"

"Seems to me like we can finally do what we want to do. Enough time and sufferin has passed. What do you want to do, Lige?"

"Danceray," he began and stopped.

Lige caught his breath and began again.

"Danceray. I love you. Always have; always will. You have been with me through all of these years. The ghost of you anyway. I've had thousands of conversations with you—course, I made up both sides a those conversations, but I tried hard to say what I thought you'd say if you had the chance. I might would get confused about the person I think you are—the one who lives inside me—and the person you are. But if you a give me the chance to learn you again—the real you—nothin would make me happier. What do you think?"

"I think that's a real pretty proposal. Let's just start over, making our future without throwing away our past. You think that's possible?"

Lige could feel his mouth stretching stupidly across his face but he did not care. He couldn't stop grinning like a fool but he didn't want to ever be any wiser than he was in that moment. And when he looked into her eyes he knew that she saw him—the him of his youth just as he saw the young girl he'd fallen in love with twenty-some-odd years before, and for good or bad that love had never turned, had never stopped; that love had bounded forth like a giant adolescent never knowing failure or expecting death.

Chapter 13

The three of them, Lige, Ivy and Danceray, settled into an easy existence that revolved around Susan and her needs. But still, the baby slept. Lige couldn't understand any creature sleeping as much as she did. Ivy continued to explain to him that it was necessary for infants to sleep and Danceray backed up her theory but that did not stop him from trying to rouse her into playfulness, into his idea of what babies were supposed to do and be. When would she discover her hands, her feet? When would she laugh out loud? Get her teeth? When would she recognize him? Or Ivy? Danceray? More important, when would she even know that she was an individual, a person, in her own right? Lige couldn't deny that he loved Susan. He would, he knew, kill everyone and anyone who tried to harm her. But he also had to admit that he was disappointed. He felt that Susan could, and should contribute more—give something back in the relationship.

"Stop bein like a big child, Lige. You got to give that baby time to grow. She ain't but two months old. What do you expect from her anyway?" Danceray said.

"I don't know. You think she's retarded?"

"Retarded? Hell! She's already turned over from her back to her stomach. She ain't retarded. She's just might be a genius for all we know."

Lige sat on the sleeping mat beside Susan watching her face for a sign, any sign, that she was aware of something other than her bottle. As he stared into her eyes, he saw the slightest shift of her head, the tiniest spark of recognition and then she smiled at him. She smiled! At him!

"Danceray! Ivy! Come here! Come look at this."

They came running, and not knowing whether what he wanted them to see was cause for alarm or celebration, they were prepared for anything. When they stood beside the mat looking at the baby, and still not knowing what they were supposed to see, Lige said, "Watch this." He tickled the bottom of Susan's foot and they all laughed watching her kick her leg straight out and seeing her smile. Sure, she had smiled before this but those times were at nothing in particular. This time, she smiled because of something external to herself and they couldn't imagine being more proud of her at any point in her future.

"Ivy, ain't your little sister just the cutest thing ever?" Danceray said.

"She sure is. I could just eat her up!"

Lige watched the two women in his life making over his little woman and thought how fortunate he was. One minute he was hungover scrounging around in the dump and the next he had a family. Danceray's eyes met his over Ivy's head and in them he saw such depth of emotion that could only be matched by his own.

"You goin to be ready to go down the mountain soon?" Lige said.

"I'm ready any time you are. Ivy, you need anything while we're in Mabry's Crossing?"

Ivy made a face at Danceray and though she didn't say anything they all knew that her expression meant she was there every single day. She lived there and, therefore, believed there was never anything in town that she needed. She picked things up as she went. Town-people never had to stock up on anything unless they came across a sale or they just wanted to in particular. Ivy handed over the keys to the four wheeler and waved Danceray and Lige away, knowing that they were going to stand there rooted in the spot where they stood in awe of Susan until she made them move on.

"Get on down the mountain before you run out a daytime. Don't forget to take that shine over to the Steak-N-Egg for Mr. Jenkins. Buy some crackers and a loaf of bread for dinner. I'm makin potato soup. Oh, and one more thing. Bring a two liter of Pepsi."

"Anything else, Ivy? For somebody never needin anything from town you sure did come up pretty darned needy all of a sudden," Lige said.

"Yeah. Go by the barber's and get that beard cut. You promised."

Lige stared at Ivy, wishing he'd stopped while he was ahead. He didn't want to trim his beard; he liked it just the way it was. But he knew that on the subject of his facial hair he was outnumbered.

"Yeah. All right. Okay. I ain't asting if there's anything else."

Lige followed Danceray over to the four wheeler. Danceray loved to ride on the back of the bike and because she did he loved it too. He glanced back one last time at the two girls under the shelter. Ivy was leaning over Susan talking to her in that language she used when she played with the baby. He didn't understand what she said but he understood from the tone what she meant. Happiness came unannounced and never admitted how long it planned to stay, and because of the realization that it could and would pack its bags and leave at a moment's notice, Lige grabbed a hold of it with both hands and with all the hospitality he could muster made it welcome. He helped Danceray onto the four wheeler and then situated himself in front of her. He already had Jenks' shine on board and a jar of peach brandy he planned to tip Doc for the beard trim and haircut. Doc wasn't really a doctor of any kind but he'd earned the nickname years ago when anybody could go to him and get stitched up after bar fights or yard fights. He was as good with a needle and cat-gut as he was with the razor and scissors.

The trip down Pouter went faster than either he or Danceray would have liked. He decided they would tend to their business in Mabry's Crossing and then light off toward the edge of town to ride aimlessly for a while. Have a little fun. Ride for no reason at all except because they wanted to. The first place they went was the Steak-N-Egg. He dropped off Jenks' bottles and he and Danceray took a seat in a corner booth. They'd missed so much over the years they spent without each other, so many activities and events that they should have done together that sometimes now they acted much younger than they were. Every now and then one or the other of them would catch someone staring at them either in judgment or support—but neither allowed either reaction from others to affect them. With the exception of the girls, they needed no one else. The waitress, a petite stringy-haired, pimply faced mouse of a girl, brought them waters and menus and walked a short distance away, giving them time to decide what they would order for lunch. Her attitude was one of polite uncaring. She had plenty of other things to worry about, real concerns. When she came back to the booth the two of them sat close together, side by side thighs touching, holding hands as if they were afraid that at any moment one or the other of them would disappear.

"What y'all goin to have?"

"I'll have a BLT and a cup of vegetable soup," Danceray said.

"I'll take the same thing and a kind word," Lige said.

"Huh?"

"Never mind. Just the sandwich and the soup. That'll be enough."

The girl noticed Danceray punch Lige in the leg in a light, sham of reprimand but she didn't understand any of what had just transpired. Old folks sure were stupid sometimes. She rolled her eyes and picked up the menus that neither Lige nor Danceray offered to hand her. *And rude*—stupid and rude. Sometimes she just felt like walking right out of this place and never looking back but she needed the money. Old folks usually tipped better than the young ones—that was one good thing about them anyway. She put them out of her mind and did her job the best she knew how and when they paid at the register, Lige handed her a dollar. When he turned toward the door, Danceray winked and slipped her another one.

Next, they decided to go ahead over to Doc's.

"Hey Baby? How about if I just get it cut to here?"

"Fine with me. Ivy's the one wantin it cut. Not me."

"That's what I can't figure out. Why's she care?"

"Beats me. But she's takin it serious."

"Let's surprise her! You care if I have Doc to shave it all the way off?"

"Course not. You got such a handsome face. Besides you can always grow it back if'n you want to."

"Ivy a be so surprised she might not even recognize me."

Just before they rounded the corner to Doc's, Blacky Jackson came out of the Farmer's Feed and Seed. Danceray put her hand on Lige's arm to keep him from advancing closer to Blacky.

"That's Blacky Jackson! Don't let him see us."

Lige did as he was told, and as he stood somewhat hidden behind a dogwood, watched the man cross the street in the opposite direction from where the two of them waited.

"Wonder what he was doin in the Feed Store? He ain't got a place around here, does he?"

"No. I would a heard about it."

"Well he's gone now. Should we go in there and ast what he bought?"

"What? Just walk in and ast? Just like that?"

"We wouldn't just walk up and ast. We could strike up a conversation with Walt. I could give him the brandy instead of Doc. Butter him up. Then casually, like we don't care, ast about Blacky. You know? Play like we don't know who he is. A black man in these parts ain't unheard of but it ain't no common sight either. What you think about that?"

"It might work. Especially with the brandy. Everybody likes a little present a that from time to time. And Walt does like to talk. Let's do it."

They came out from behind the sparse cover of the dogwood and went up the steps to the feed store. Once inside, Lige stopped to look at a lawnmower. He didn't have a use for one but it seemed like the manly thing to do. Walt walked over to them instead of them having to make the approach, making it seem like they didn't have a motive for coming in. Good. Now he could say he was just window shopping, looking around at the new models.

"Elijah Worley. I ain't seen you in a month of Sundays. Where you been keepin yourself? How you been?"

Lige hated it when a person asked multiple questions of him, not giving him time to answer one before another was fired at him. Usually in those cases he didn't answer any of them.

"How's Sarah doin, Walt?"

"She's good. Good. A little tired these days after the operation."

Shit! Wrong question. Lige was unaware of an illness or operation.

"Here. That's why I brought you this peach brandy. Blackberry would've maybe been more toothsome to her but that batch didn't last much past the week after it fermented. You know when the blackberries're gone they're gone. Tell her we ast about her, okay?"

"Will do! You lookin for a mower?"

"Nah, not really. Just saw this one from the porch and wanted to see it up close."

Danceray realized that Lige couldn't find an opening to ask the question.

"Walt, we noticed a black man comin out as we come up. Who's he, do you know?"

"I don't know him, know him. But I've seen him goin around with Tater and Eustus Jr. Come in here today and bought syringes. No law against buyin em but what's he need em for is what I wonder."

"Maybe Tater's shootin the pigs up with something? Who knows?"

"More like Tater's shootin himself up with something," Lige said.

"Yeah. You got that shit right, man. Tater's so stupid you just got to let him be Tater's all I know."

The three of them laughed and Lige began to make his way to the door. Danceray followed close behind him.

"Give Sarah our love, Walt. And tell her if'n she needs anything to let me know. Anything at all. Hear me?"

"I sure will. Thanks Danceray. Sarah'll be glad to hear it."

They walked through the door, the bell jangling behind them.

"Syringes? What the hell?" Danceray said.

"Really. What's a stranger to these parts with no land and no animals out buyin syringes for?"

"I don't like it one bit, Lige. Don't make sense to me."

"Let's go get Doc to clean me up and then on back up the mountain."

"Good idea. I want to check on the girls."

They looked at one another, knowingly but neither spoke. Lige had a bad feeling and though he tried to push it to the side, tried to brush it off, the feeling persisted. Something was brewing. And he didn't like it at all. It was one thing if he knew what was going on, what he was up against but when there was only a nagging half-formed thought, there was nothing to go after. Nothing to try and stop because there was no way to know the enemy, no way to identify the demons. He had been so pleased after their retreat but now it appeared they once more advanced, stronger and more numerous than before. An army of demons. And any time he reached to touch them to eliminate them they dissipated like a ghostly, foggy form and then regrouped and in a more sophisticated shape crossed the lines of safety.

"Danceray? I don't think it's a good idea to even stop for my shave. Let's go on home. See to the children."

"What's Ivy goin to say when we come up with you still wearin that hair on your face? Assumin everything's all right there."

"That's a chance I'll have to take. Their safety's more important than anything else. Let's stop in the Dollar General and get the crackers and bread and then go on home."

"What was that other thing she said to get?"

"Pepsi. That was all, right?"

"I think so. Let's hurry Lige. I got a God-awful, feelin in my stomach."

Chapter 14

Even with their portentous trepidation, neither Lige nor Danceray were prepared for the sight that met them as soon as they rode over the crest of the final hill bringing them out into the clearing of the shelter. Danceray, who like almost all mountain women, possessed great inner strength and immense outer stoicism, began to wail, shrieking words that both made sense and did not. *Gone. Children. All we have. Lost. Never forgive. Tater.* Lige wanted to fall apart too but he knew that he did not have that luxury. He looked from place to place unable to keep his eyes on one spot for more than a few seconds. He was helpless. Thoughts of Eller and the baby crashed into his mind, invading spaces that he needed to keep vacant—to fill with a new hurt, a new plan. Lige was aware of a bawling, screeching yelp gathering itself up from the seat of his being and working its way to his throat but his throat was blocked. His throat was a structure through which nothing could pass out or in. In fact, he could barely breathe and was all breath at once. He didn't know how long he could handle all of the contradictions surrounding him. Was life supposed to be this way? Full of *yes, buts.* All he knew at the moment was that he was responsible for these three females that God or somebody else had entrusted to him. Susan. Ivy. And Danceray. They were his life; they were his family. His!

There was no sign of Susan or Ivy, however, and no matter where he looked there was only emptiness. He needed to comfort Danceray; he knew that. Any man would comfort his woman, right? But he couldn't. He was, in that moment, as incapable as an armless man. His hands might as well be gone. He couldn't pick up the baby with them, he couldn't hold Danceray with them, and he couldn't reach out to muss Ivy's hair with them. His hands were tied, or paralyzed or cut away from his body—it didn't matter which—as far as he was concerned. There was nothing for him to do and everything for him to do. But what does one do when one doesn't know what to do? And then he heard a click in his mind, just behind his right ear, and just as surely as if he'd heard the click of a key in a lock. The underground room! Maybe Ivy made it to the room with Susan. Were they down there? In his mind, he pictured Ivy down under the ground, holding Susan close to her body, huddled in fear and confusion—not knowing what to do next. Whether to stay put or to come out. But first, he needed to at least get Danceray to sit down, and as much as he hated to admit it, he needed to make her shut up. He couldn't think straight with her circling the parameter of the camp, pulling her hair and screeching like a banshee. To him, she sounded half-specter, half-mountain cat, not like a woman at all. He would have never believed had he been told at any time in the past that he would ever want her voice silenced, but now he knew it was true. He wanted, needed, her stillness.

Lige went to her, put a hand on her shoulder and felt her leap under his touch. He took her in his arms and crushed her smallness into his large frame. Still, she fought against him, against everything, and against nothing. Her children were in danger, perhaps dead and she would not be calmed. Everything in him, everything in his psychological make-up, was in opposition when he struck her across the face and shook her violently. There was no fear in her eyes, no trembling in her body, no rebuke in her voice. He was certain that she knew why he slapped her and he watched as she slightly shook her head and then cocked it to the side a quarter turn like an old hound after forced composure not understanding the situation surrounding the fit. She was no fool. She was a pain-filled creature. He led her to a seat under the shelter and gave her the bottle of shine. She took the liquor from him and drank straight from the bottle, wiping her mouth with the back of her hand before she spoke.

"Elijah? I need my babies!"

"I know. Me too. We a find em, I swear it to you."

"I can't stand it! I can't. I just can't."

"Baby, just sit here for a minute. Just be calm. I need to look in the room."

"I'll go with you."

Lige didn't want her to follow him down into the underground room; he didn't know what he might find down there. He wasn't sure he could handle the worst but he was certain that she couldn't. He had to protect her from the worst.

"Just stay right here. I'll be right back."

Before he walked away from her, he bent to kiss her gently on the cheek in an effort of reassurance. He went to the trapdoor, noticed the brush and dirt had been scraped away, and with a trembling hand and a quaking heart pulled the handle toward him. He lit the lantern that he'd left near the opening and made his way down into the cavernous room. Susan and Ivy were not there. But still, his heart held out hope. When he had finished digging

141

the main room, he had veered off to the right opening into a small rectangle wide enough for a person to lie down and deep enough to stand with his shoulders in a stoop. The small area had been an afterthought, and even as he'd dug it he had no idea why he did but afterward realized that if a person didn't know of its existence then they wouldn't be able to see it clearly from the main room. Lige would be forever unsure whether he vomited or saw the bundle in the corner first. Susan. He made his way quickly to her. *Dear God in heaven don't let her be dead. Don't let her be dead. She looks dead. She ain't movin. Don't let her be dead or kill me here where I stand.* As soon as he touched her, feeling the warmth coming from her miniature, perfect body he felt hope rise in him like syrup from a tapped maple. He couldn't see her clearly for he'd left the lantern where he stood upon sight of her but he felt her twist in the rapture of a yawn. *Damn! Thank you God for making Susan love to sleep! I swear I a never complain about that again! I swear it. You sure do know what you're doin God—keepin everything goin like it's posed to. Thank you God. Thank you!* He clutched Susan to him never wanting to put her down, never wanting to leave her open to danger, again. How could a body protect those he loved at all times, at all costs? *Am I man enough for this?* He roughly wiped a tear from the corner of his eye, not allowing it to make its intended course. There was no time for crying now. He had to step up to this here in front of him. If he'd found Susan down here alone, then that meant the room did its job—for her. But Ivy was not with her. Ivy was gone. He felt more tears pushing at the backs of his eyes, burning like hot pin-pricks, struggling to make their way out, for relief. Pent up emotion demanding release. But he couldn't let loose of all of it now. He had to hold it all in, force it together, and make a way. Nothing would ever be pleasing or even agreeable to him again if he lost Ivy. He picked up the lantern by the thin wire handle and swung himself and Susan out of the ground. He was in front of Danceray and handing Susan off to her in the space of time it took to let out his held breath.

Danceray took her from him, greedily pulling the summer blanket from around her, frantically removing her Onesie, her little booties, checking the soft, silky baby-flesh for injury. Finding none, she relaxed and smiled up at Lige.

"Thank God! Oh Lige, what would we've done if …"

Her voice quivered and stopped, the tears spilling out of her eyes and rolling big and fat down her face. Lige watched her shoulders moving furiously up and down and her free hand clapped over her mouth in effort to gain control. Finally, she gathered her composure enough to stare around the camp.

"Where's Ivy? We need to get Susan changed and fed."

"I don't know."

If Lige had been born a different man, then maybe he would know what words to use. That other man would use tact and discretion when giving information such as this. He would be able to say what he now needed to say without raising alarm—to say it while gaining and keeping control. That other man would be smooth, with delicate judgment. But Lige had not been born a different man. Lige was Lige, and Lige possessed none of the qualities of that other man.

"What do you mean, you don't know?"

"She's gone. Not here. She done good hidin Susan the way she done. But she didn't hide herself in time, I reckon."

"She ain't dead, is she? Oh my God, Lige! Please tell me she ain't layin down there dead."

"She ain't down there dead. She just ain't down there at all. She's gone. Somebody took her. She'd a never left Susan by herself."

Lige allowed his gaze to travel across the entirety of the campsite taking in everything. Ivy had started the pot of potato soup. The pot was turned over on its side with its milky liquid and chunks of potatoes spilled on the ground. Everything under the shelter had been molested. The bed mat was flipped and tossed so that it lay half-in and half-out of the shelter. The nightstand was turned over with all its drawers and their contents strewn everywhere. There was no sign of struggle really, just clumsy, ham-fisted rummaging. He permitted his mind to retrace his trip down to the underground room. There was no sign of struggle there either. Just Susan placed in the corner as easily as if she'd been put to bed. There'd been a sacrifice. Ivy had given herself up to him, or them, in order to keep Susan, the baby she'd come to love as a sister, maybe even in her own way, a daughter, safe. Ivy had played her hand and won but what had she been dealt in its place? What cards did she now hold? He thought of the old .22 and hoping against hope that it was still among his possessions went to get it. He should have known it would be gone. He still had the Bowie knife tucked into his boot where he always carried it but he knew he might not be able to get close enough to use a knife. He had to get another gun and this one needed to be a larger caliber—needed to be more powerful and more reliable an aim. .22s were the kind of gun used for up close and personal—a bullet in the side of the head, maybe just behind an ear where the tiny projectile whirred its way in and then twisted and twirled through the soft brain matter, ultimately doing as much damage as any other shot would. But if he worried about getting close enough to use the knife, a .22 was only slightly better. He was out of touch with where to get such things because he hadn't needed them in a long while. *Think, Lige, think! Where can I get a gun? An unregistered piece. And fast. From someone who knows how to keep their trap shut too.* Lige didn't want to add unnecessary murder on top of necessary. Surely, some of his shine customers dealt in guns, weapons, drugs and or other gear and vice. Of course! Strick Coalson. Strick had served in the military. Which branch was it? Oh yeah, that's right, he was a Jarhead. No. it was the ARMY. Now he spent most of his time dropping acid and selling or trading guns and ammo. Still wore his fatigues; still thought he fought a war. Maybe he did. There was more than one kind of war. People fight them all the time, sometimes never even leaving the shadow of a mountain; he knew that for true and sure.

"Danceray? How fast can you get Susan fed and changed? We got to go."

"Purdy fast. Where we goin though?"

"I got to go see a man about a gun. I ain't goin to lie to you neither. Could be dangerous for you and Susan but I think it's more dangerous to stay here. You think you should go on back to Salter?"

"No. I don't. We're in this together. Get me a gun too while we're at it. I can shoot. I'll be needin a .38. with a small grip. Five shot'll do—six'll be better though."

For the first time since they'd laid eyes on Blacky Jackson earlier in the day, they both laughed and though their laughter was a tad too loud and long, still, they laughed. Lige saw it as another pact between him and Danceray. They would keep this family they'd pieced together, together at all costs.

"I wish we had somebody to leave Susan with," she said.

That one comment was the only sign that either of them thought they might fail in any way. Lige thought seriously about what she said, flipping through his mind like cards on a rolodex—not many cards to be sure but a few.

"Strick's ol' lady might watch her. We'll see when we get there. Otherwise, we'll just have to leave her in the basket."

Danceray worked quickly making the bottle and changing the baby's diaper.

"We goin all the way up Pinter?"

"No. Strick ain't lived on Pinter for several years now. Lives out by the lake. Over on the water-shed side."

"Good. That's a might closer."

Danceray stood with Susan, ready to go and she and Lige smiled strained smiles at one another. Lige moved to her, took her in his arms and kissed her allowing all the fierce emotion in him to course through him and into her. They were a two-person team, getting ready to work together on the most vital, imperative undertaking imaginable and Lige knew there was not another person alive he'd prefer to have his back than Danceray. He trusted her above all others. And success was more likely because she was the only person who wanted what he wanted as much, and probably if it was possible even more, than he did. He released her, saying, "Ready?"

"Never been more ready in my life! Let's do this!"

He couldn't hide the smile that her words brought to his lips.

"Let's go get our girl! Yeah!"

Clearly they had the necessary enthusiasm but where was the plan?

"Seriously though Danceray, we got any idea what to do after we get them guns?"

Momentarily, Danceray lost her zest. What did they do next? They needed a plan. Ivy could be anywhere. *Oh my God! She could be dead.* Danceray forced the thoughts from her mind. Where should they start? And almost before she asked herself the question, she had the answer.

"As a matter of fact, I do. We need to go to Susan's grandma's house. What's her name? Ilene? No. Aileen. Ivy said she lives right down there in Mabry's Crossing. At the end of Poteat street. Let's start there."

"Damned good idea. She's the one talkin about some older, black-haired guy in the first place. She might have some other information."

Chapter 15

The trip out to Strick's house had been easy. Almost as soon as they started out on the four wheeler, it seemed they were at his back door. Lige rapped loudly on the screen-door knowing that it was still early enough in the evening not to be considered rude to do so. A woman who appeared to be in her fifties came to the back door and it took Lige a few minutes to recognize her as Strick's wife, Loretta, who was in fact just barely past thirty. What had caused her to age so severely, he would never know. Drugs? Disease? Just hard living?

"Can I do for you, Lige Worley?"

"Just lookin for Strick. He around?"

She stuck her bare foot through the opening at the bottom of the screen-door and pointed with it toward the shed in the back yard. Lige noticed her toenails had once been painted with red polish that clung to the surface in ragged, sporadic strokes, as if loathe to let go. She took a long draw off a Kool, causing her cheeks to sink into the open, toothless backside of her mouth and then exhaled the harsh smoke before she spoke.

"Strick's in the shed. Where he stays. He should just pack his bags and move in out there," Loretta laughed, "But hey! Listen. Don't get'im in no trouble. He ain't been off probation a month yet this time."

"We ain't aimin to get Strick in trouble. We're not up to no good. Not really," Lige said.

"Loretta? Can you watch my little niece here for me? Just for a little while."

Loretta peeped out the door at the picnic basket.

"You got a baby in there?"

"Yeah. She ain't no trouble. I promise."

"Well, I don't know about none a that."

Loretta coughed violently.

"Really. She sleeps almost all the time," Lige said.

And for the second time that day, he was thankful for Susan's sleepy nature.

"I ain't been feelin too good. You say she's sleepin?"

"How about if we bring you a candy bar and soda pop when we get back."

"I reckon it'll be all right then."

Danceray stood smiling like an angel having the power over all the world's troubles.

"What kind you want?"

"Bring me one of them king-size Butterfingers and a Mountain Dew. Twenty ounce one."

Lige handed her the basket.

"Now, she ate about thirty minutes ago. Shouldn't be hungry till after we come back. If'n she does there's a full bottle in there. Just heat it up a ..."

"Lige Worley shut your mouth. I done had four babies and been takin care a them all this time. I think I can take care of this one just fine without you tellin me how."

"I know it, Loretta. I know it. Wouldn't'a ast you if'n I didn't know you could do it."

Loretta made no reply; she merely took the basket and stepped back inside the house with it. Lige and Danceray made their way across the back yard and Lige was the first to speak.

"You think we should go back and get her?"

"No, I don't think we should."

"Something's wrong with Loretta. What if something happens to Susan while we're gone?"

"Ain't nothin wrong with her that'll make her hurt the baby. Life's just beat that woman down. Life and all its disappointments. Susan'll be fine."

"You sure about that?"

"Yep. Let it go, Honeybear. We got other things to tend to right now."

"Yeah you're right. She'll be fine. Just ain't never left her nowhere before."

Lige and Danceray walked up to the door of the shed, knocked and waited for permission to enter. Strick finally slid the door to the side and stood staring at them, not recognizing either of them for a long minute. Lige stepped forward, expecting to be let inside but when he did Strick stepped forward too. From where Danceray stood, they looked like a pantomime of two men pretending to be one man in a mirror. She almost laughed but wasn't quite ready for laughing. Right then, she just wanted this part of the evening to pass on by—be done with.

"Well, I be a sumbtich. Lige! Where the hell you been man?"

Strick moved forward and clasped Lige's shoulder, digging in deeply and shaking him back and forth. Lige was so much taller than Strick that the shorter man had to stretch his arm fully to complete the gesture of friendship. Strick wore a plaid bathrobe, with a pair of cut-off, fatigues—the legs uneven, and one navy sock and one black stuffed into in a pair of flip-flops. On his face, he wore a pair of prescription eyeglasses, one of the arms taped back together with shiny, white medical tape. Strick's eyes appeared magnified behind the glasses.

"Oh, I just been up on Pouter. You know that from buyin shine."

Lige didn't understand banter or small talk and he was a little bit nervy with it now.

"I know that! I know where you really been. I just meant you ain't never down here. You know? Like, why're you here? That kind of thing. Not a real question, man, damn!"

"Oh yeah. Okay. Guess that makes sense. We need a couple guns. Don't matter if they're hot. Don't want no paperwork."

"Okay. All right. What kind of guns."

Strick was straight down to business then.

"I reckon a .357 and a .38. And a box a .38s since they'll go for both."

Danceray thought the less said, the better.

"We're goin target shootin, Strick. Won't that be fun?"

"Fun? Yeah. Yeah. That's always lots a fun. I'd go with y'all if'n I didn't have so much to do around here."

Strick spread his hands out in front of him palms up as if to say, *See all this shit I got to do?* He went behind a candy counter, he'd probably gotten from the IGA—the only grocery store Mabry's Crossing had. Well, that is until the Dollar General came in. They sell groceries too, just not as many as the IGA.

"What is Pearl Harbor, mother-fucker!"

Lige looked at Danceray in alarm. Strick screaming out about Pearl Harbor while handling firearms didn't appeal to him in the least.

"Pearl Harbor! You should a said it."

Lige leaned across the counter, reducing the space between them to maybe an inch, if that.

"Strick, man, that shit ain't funny."

"Huh? What shit?"

"Screamin about bombin and shit. Cut it out."

Strick doubled over in a fit of laughter.

"I ain't tryin to be funny, man! It's Jeopardy. The answer was *Japanese attack on America*, so the question's *what is Pearl Harbor*."

Lige looked around the room, located the television set on the top shelf of a gun cabinet, and saw Alex Trebec before he put the whole thing together.

"Stupid fuck should a got that. Hell, everyone a my kids would've."

"Yeah. He should a got it."

Strick, serious again, laid the two guns and the box of ammunition on the counter between them.

"Four-twenty and three-seventy-five. Pay in cash and you can have em for four and three-fifty."

"I'll give you three-fifty and three and as much free shine as you can handle for the rest of your life. How bout that?"

"Lige? You lie to your friends and I'll lie to mine but let's don't lie to each other. You in some kind a trouble? You need some help? I ain't that busy."

"I got some business, yeah. And I appreciate the offer but you don't want in on this, trust me."

"All right man, if you say so. But you know I'll go with you. Danceray can stay right here with Loretta. Might be safer that a way."

Lige glanced at Danceray to see what her thoughts were and she shook her head almost without moving it.

"Thanks again, but we got it. Best help you can give us is to forget you ever saw us this evenin. You do that for me?"

"You bet I will and I'll do you one better. See that rusted out truck over there by the apple tree? It's registered to somebody down in Georgia, or maybe it's Alabama. Hell, for all I know that person might even be dead by now. Take it and leave that little cycle here. Pick it up when you come back. You follow what I say?"

"Yeah, I follow you. And I thank you. We got a deal on the money?"

"I got a even better deal than that one. Borrow the guns; bring em back when you bring the truck back, pay for the ammo. Deal?"

"Why would you do that?"

"Cause something tells me you won't need the guns after tonight. And whatever you do with em—and I don't want to know what that is—won't nobody ever suspect that two guns sittin here coolin in this here cabinet ever did no work. I *will* take the deal with the shine though."

Lige nodded his head, touched by the way Strick wanted to help without even knowing the story, but then wondered if he might be setting him up somehow. How would such a set-up work? He decided it wouldn't work. Strick was sincere.

"That's a deal."

"But you'll have to clean em when you come back. They'll be your fingerprints, after all. I wouldn't want to be blamed for missin one."

Lige handed over the money for the ammunition and realized that he just got the use of a truck and two guns, the means to carry out the deed before them for thirty bucks and a lifetime supply of liquor. Most people were good or wanted to be.

"Hold on a minute, buddy. I almost forgot something I brought you."

Lige went to the four wheeler and when he came back in the shed, he handed Strick a jar of peach brandy.

"See that recliner over there? That's where I'm goin to spend the rest of the evenin; fact is, I been there all night already, drinkin this good ol' peach brandy. This peach brandy, I bought from you up on Pouter a few weeks ago. And by the time I'm done, I'll probably even eat a peach or two out of it. Won't know who's come or gone all night. And don't never say I said it but Loretta's good with what's right in front of her but once something's out a her sight it's out a her mind too."

Lige smiled and turned to go, Danceray following close behind him, when Strick spoke again.

"Lige, Danceray!"

They looked back and saw Strick standing by the chair, grinning and holding his right hand over his brows in a salute.

"Go with God, friends. Go with God."

Lige nodded his head once in the downward motion and stepped out into the darkness of the yard. They settled into the bench seat of the Ford pickup and looked at each other for only a brief moment before Lige reached to the right of the steering column, trusting the keys to be there. He turned the keys and the engine, while not exactly purring, started up immediately.

"Well, Strick thinks of everything, don't he? Danceray said.

"Yep. Bet if'n he hadn't gotten out a the service, he'd be a four star general by now."

Chapter 16

They wheeled the truck onto Poteat, and before they made it past the first house Lige cut the lights and slowed the engine. He wasn't sure he needed to be so guarded at this point but he wasn't sure he didn't either. Better to be cautious. The truck rolled on almost silently, except for a couple times when the rubber tires turned over stray gravel, until they came to a stop at the curb in front of Aileen's house. Rhonda's mother meant they were close to an answer, some kind of answer, at least they hoped they were because if they reached a dead end here then they wouldn't know what to do, where to go, next. Everything rode on this one conversation with this one person. Lige's brain unexpectedly threw him a curve ball. He knew that Aileen was Susan's grandmother; he had known she was the whole time—ever since Ivy had told him about the woman, that is. But now when faced with actually meeting Aileen, he worried that he would say something about Susan. What if she found out about her and decided to take her from him, from them? He could not allow that. He would never give Susan over to anyone whether they were her flesh and blood or not. Susan didn't belong to her grandmother—Susan didn't even know her.

"Danceray! No matter what happens in here, no matter what anybody says, *do not* mention Susan. I mean it! Even if she brings up the baby. Her pregnant child. Wantin to know what happened to the baby. Do not by deed or word let her know we have her."

Danceray's face paled and he knew she hadn't thought all of this through yet either. Who did they think they were? How would they ever find Ivy? *Stop it! Stop it! Failure is not a option!*

"You're right. Thank God Loretta agreed to keep her."

They got out of the truck, quietly closing the doors behind them and made their way up the front walk. Lige took in the appearance of the yard the best he could in the dark. There was something that bothered him about it right off the bat. Right from jump. Aileen's yard was full of flowers. There were flowers in every color, size and shape imaginable. There were hanging baskets on the front porch—three of them. There were flowers growing from the middles of tires set out in the yard, and up from the ground against the border and around the sides of the house. And every single flower he saw was wilted, thirsty—some of the heads dead, needing a pinch. Who could love flowers as much as she must and sit back and watch as they died such a slow death as these did. A bud without water was the equivalent of a person slowly suffocating from a lack of oxygen in imminent death. Perhaps Aileen was sick, confined to bed. But even then, didn't she have a phone? Couldn't she ask someone to water these pitiful flowers and plants?

"Stay close, Danceray. And keep your hand on that gun. Something's wrong here."

Danceray didn't answer but he felt her stiffen behind him as they stepped up onto the front porch. There was a table lamp burning inside. He could see it through the picture window. And when he looked further into the back of the house through the window, he saw a light on above the kitchen sink. He extended an index finger and pressed the doorbell. He didn't have to wonder if it worked; he could hear it from where he stood. They waited. No one came to the door. He rang the bell again. Still no one came. It was too early for bedtime.

"Let's go around to the back."

They stepped lightly down the front steps and made their way to the back door. There was no doorbell back there so he made a fist and banged on the wooden frame. Again they waited. Lige tried the door and unlike in television shows or movies, the lock was not set. The door swung open easily but noisily. Someone should put some WD-40 on those hinges. They walked in, single file, and maneuvered around a fairly new washer and dryer and an exercise bike. As soon as they turned into the kitchen the God-awfullest stench blasted into their faces like a squall of salt-wind off the ocean.

"My God, Lige! What the hell is that smell?"

"I don't know. Smells like a guts-out, dead cat!"

They made their way into and through the front room and finding no one there started down the hallway. The house was one of those ranch-style ones with the kitchen and front room on one end and down the hallway three bedrooms and a bath. Lige felt the impact of their intrusion and decided it would be best to call out. Let Aileen know someone was in the house. But even as he had the thought, he held out no hope that she was alive. The courtesy he wanted to extend to her was merely a morbid formality because Lige was almost certain that the odor was Aileen. When they had looked into all but the last bedroom, his lungs bursting for breath but unwilling to take in any of the stale, reeking air, he mustered all of his courage and pushed open the door. The body of who he assumed to be Aileen lay on the bed, blackened and bulging with the lewdness of a vile and unnatural death. One eye was open and staring lifeless at the ceiling and the other was squeezed tightly shut. How was that possible? Either you died with your eyes open or you died with them closed. He'd never seen or heard of a dead body with one eye open. Unless... unless, you died with a swollen, blacked eye. Then you could die with one eye open and one closed. Lige held his nose and kept his mouth unyieldingly closed and marched quickly into the room, to the wastebasket near the bed. He hurriedly rifled through the various items therein. When he pulled out his hand, he held the item for which he'd searched. Easy as that! Tater was a stupid, stupid man who thought he was oh, so smart. He turned to Danceray whose face was not only ashen but also visibly shaking. He'd seen a quivering chin, and he'd witnessed a trembling lip but never had he seen the flesh of a person's face actually shake. There was no movement of the head, just a shaking face. The sight was frightful and he wanted her to make it stop.

"Elijah? I don't understand. What does this mean? Blacky only bought the needle today. We saw him. We saw him come out of the feed store. Walt said it. This woman's been dead a while. But he only bought it today, Lige."

Lige wasn't the smartest man in the world, he'd said it before and he'd known it for a long time, but when Danceray asked him those questions the answers sprung into his head full-blown. It was like the rubber mallet

161

struck his patella—his knee-muscle—and the information went straight to his brain, skipping his spinal cord.

"The needle Blacky bought today was for Ivy, Danceray."

"But he wouldn't have been able to beat us up Pouter and back down again without us crossin his path. That don't make sense."

"Tater could though. He could a sent Blacky for the needle and went after Ivy by himself."

"And he went after *Ivy*? Are we sure about that? Maybe he really only wanted Susan and found Ivy instead. How would he even know about Ivy, Lige?"

The full impact of her words socked Lige in the gut with such force that he fell to his knees there in Aileen's bedroom and unable to pick himself back up from the carpeted floor, he crawled and scrambled on all fours all the way through the house, making his way to the front door and fresh air. For the second time that evening he vomited. Danceray came up behind him and placed her cool hand on the back of his neck and with the other hand rubbed the top of his head, smoothing the hair of his bangs away from his forehead which was covered with a thick, sickening sweat. The sweat of panicked, dreadful terror. She eased herself down beside him and put her arm around his shoulder. Danceray had the answers now; she would step up and take over.

"Lige? Listen to me. We found out what we needed to know. Aileen's dead. Tater killed her just like he killed Rhonda. We don't know, and we don't have to know, why. All we got to know is he did it. The needle proves he did it.

Now. He has Ivy; we can be almost one hundred percent sure of that. That brings us to the question of why he would take Ivy. The answer to that is that he wants Susan. We can find them before he kills her if we think like he thinks. He needs to keep Ivy alive long enough to make her tell him about the baby. Ivy won't tell him. She's strong. She's ours."

"What if the bastard's already killed her? What then? Huh?"

He almost screamed the word *huh* at her without even much awareness of having raised his voice. She didn't let such a little thing bother her. He would never speak to her in such a way under normal circumstances. And these circumstances were anything but normal.

"We can't think like that right now. We got to go find our girl. I think first thing to do is check around here. See if there's anywhere they could be keepin her. They wouldn't waste time headin back up the ridge if they didn't have to. This is the perfect place with Aileen dead."

And since Lige had no other plan, he allowed Danceray to lead him. To decide their next move. They went back around the house from the opposite side and scanned the property. There was a detached garage back there close to the house but there was no one hiding there with Ivy or otherwise. The garage was one of those open ones that people bought more as a shelter for their cars than anything else. Like a canopy. They passed by it and staying close to the house moved past the back deck and the door they'd earlier entered the house through. Just as they made it almost to the corner of the opposite side, Lige glanced down toward a sliver of light. There was the top of a window there with the remainder of it buried underground. A galvanized dome curved around the front of the window so that in order to peep through the panes one had to bend down almost to laying on their stomach to see anything. And when he did just that a familiar, elusive fragrance filled his nose and coursed into his sinuses. What was that scent? Where had he smelled it before?

Danceray was beside him looking into the basement with him. They watched as events unfolded that made modern movies seem trite and affable. This, real life, scene was grisly, and repugnant. There was no dramatic pause, no music in the background instructing the viewer how to feel, what to believe. He moved to cover Danceray's eyes but she pushed him away, wildly. Her family was down there. Tater not only by marriage but also through time served—with him and the rest of his clan. And though she'd been prepared to murder him with the .38 she carried with her watching what now happened was a different story. Eustus Jr., her nephew, held a gun in one hand—looked to be a .22, maybe Lige's gun?—and in the other hand about a four foot length of garden hose. They could hear the noises coming up from the basement, muffled as if they came from a great distance, perhaps through a culvert or a span of ducts, but clearly discernible. Another contradiction.

"Why'd you do it, Daddy? Ever damn thang I ever had, you took! You always take it from me. Don't matter if'n I love it or want it or need it. No sir! That only makes you want it more."

Lige felt Danceray flinch with the discharge of a bullet which found its way into one of Tater's outstretched legs, just below the knee. And then he felt as she recoiled after each time Eustus Jr. brought the hose down against his father. Tater mistakenly but instinctively raised his hands to protect his face and the bones cracking within the right hand sounded like dry kindling catching a flame. Pop, pop, crack. The noise without the knowledge of the cause was bearable, innocuous—bland even, but awareness of the breaking of bones made the stomach tilt. Tater's face was swollen and purpled with bruises, his legs riddled with so many bullet holes that he couldn't have stood or scrambled away if he tried but something told Lige, made him believe, that Tater had not tried to escape. Eustus Jr. reloaded the gun and Lige couldn't help but notice that the young man's hands did not tremble with nerves. He was in total command of his body if not his mind. But then again maybe he did control his wits.

"You knowed I loved Rhonda. You knowed we was goin to get married. You knowed all a that. But did you care, you sumbitch? No! You found out about her and moved in like you was some young buck. Like you would ever be something she wanted. She hated you. And I was too skeered to stop you. You fuckin bully. Everbody hates you—even Mama! We all hate you."

Eustus Jr. shot again, once in each leg.

"That's right boy! Stand up for yourself. Bout time you was a man about something! Hit me again! Come on; bring it on!"

Tater laughed disgustingly and then choked, dark, foamy blood gurgling from his mouth and nose.

"But here's one thang you need to know, old man! That baby ain't yours. No chance a that. That baby's mine. Mine and Rhonda's. And now that I know she's alive you got to damn sure die cause I ain't never lettin you get to her like you did those two babies a Mama's you throwed in the river like they was cats you was drownin. You didn't think I knowed about them, did you? You ain't gettin your hands on my baby. You hear me?"

Tater didn't answer Eustus Jr. Tater looked up at him and grinned. Eustus Jr. held the gun to his father's temple. Lige saw Eustus Jr. hesitate for only a moment, enough time to allow Tater to jerk the gun from his hand, put the barrel in his own mouth and pull the trigger with the thumb of his left hand. There was no blood or gore, no brains spattering on the wall behind him. One second he was alive and grinning and the next he was dead and not grinning. Absurdly, Lige was thankful Tater's eyes were closed. He stood and helped Danceray up from the ground. There was no outside door to the basement so he figured there had to only be a way in or out from the inside of the house. He hadn't seen it when he'd been inside but then he hadn't been looking for one either. He took Danceray's hand and together they walked back around to the front of the house. They'd only stood on the porch for a minute or two when Eustus Jr. came bounding through the front door. Distraught, he hadn't even seen them standing to the right of the front door. He sat down on the top step and screamed the most silent scream Lige had ever heard. Good. He didn't want the neighbors to be alerted. Of course, they might have already heard the gunshots but it was doubtful. They would have to involve the police before the night was over anyway, but first he had to find out about Ivy. He stepped over behind Eustus

166

Jr. and placed a heavy hand on his shoulder at about the exact moment, the boy noticed the rusted out Ford in front of the house. Lige sat down heavily to his right and Danceray sat on the edge of the step on the other side of him. She slipped her arm around him and hugged him to her.

"Aunt Danceray. I done something awful."

"Shhh. I know. I know. It's goin to be all right."

"No ma'am, it ain't never goin to be all right. I done killed my daddy."

"Hush now, baby, and listen to me. Your daddy had a killin comin to him every which way he turned. And it might not seem like it now but it's a good thing, in a way, that you're the one that done it. Lige and me was comin to kill him too. But you needed to get all that hate out a you or you was never goin to have a chance at nothin. Not nothin in this world."

"I'm goin to jail though. What kind a chance is that at anything?"

"What you goin to jail for, son?" Lige said.

"For killin my daddy. Ain't you been listenin to me?"

"Yeah. I reckon I have. But I watched the whole thing. You give him a beatin that would a killed most men, but you didn't kill him. He shot himself through the mouth. I'll testify to that."

"Y'all seen it?"

"Just about every bit of it. Ugly sight. Damn near unbearable to watch. But anybody that knowed Tater Shifflett'll be on your side, and *that* includes the law."

Lige realized in the same way a word will come to a person once he relaxes and stops thinking about it, what the fragrance he'd caught earlier was. Ivy's perfume. Ivy had been right there either in or near the basement.

"How can you love somebody and hate em at the same time?"

"Happens all the time. Hate ain't nothin but love turned on its back. Now, can you answer us something?"

"If I can, I will."

"You come across a girl this evening with blonde hair, name of Ivy?"

"Sure did. I've knowed Ivy my whole life. Went to school together. In a way, she started all this. But I don't guess that's really the truth. Daddy was goin to kill her the same way he killed Aileen. Shoot her full a heroin with that cow needle. Overdose her. He roughed her up a little bit before I got here. Not too bad. Just smacked her a few times. That's when I found out about Susan still bein alive. That's when I went crazy, I guess."

"Where's Ivy now? She still alive?"

Lige was afraid to ask the question, afraid of the answer but he had to know. His nerves couldn't take much more.

"Yeah, she's fine. She ast Blacky to take her back up Pouter to get the baby. Said she left her there hidden somewhere when Daddy come up on em."

"Blacky!?" Danceray said.

"Yeah Blacky. He's a good friend a mine. Think he's got his eyes on Ivy too."

"But we saw him today comin out a the feed store with a syringe!"

"Daddy's been usin him to do his biddin. Blacky didn't know. Daddy told him he had to vaccinate the cows. Blacky don't even know Daddy ain't got no cows. Daddy gave him enough money to get a cheeseburger at the Steak-N-Egg if he'd get that needle while he was in town. Blacky don't like Mama's cookin too much. Do about anything for a burger and fries."

Danceray stood abruptly.

"Let's go fellas. Ivy's goin to pitch a fit when she gets all the way up Pouter and finds Susan gone."

The three of them walked on shaky legs to the truck. Danceray seated herself in the middle, spreading her legs so the gearstick had free range of movement. Eustus Jr. finally processed the information about Susan not being on Pouter.

"Where's my baby if'n she ain't where Ivy left her?"

"Loretta's watchin her. Lige pull in over there to the Dollar General."

"I'm already on it."

Lige went in the store and was back out again in less than three minutes. He held a king-sized Butterfinger in one hand and a twenty ounce Mountain Dew in the other. Danceray took them from him and smiled at Eustus Jr.

"Babysittin payment."

"Oh. Should we go by the police station first?"

"No sir. You're goin to meet your little baby and we're goin to find out for sure that Ivy's all right first. Then we'll all go to the station together."

"Aunt Danceray? I don't want to sound like a bad daddy right off the bat, but I don't know how to take care of a baby or nothin like that. I mean I want to be in her life an all but I can't do it by myself. Mama's got a house full already. And after she finds out what I done, well, she might not want me around no more anyway."

Lige thought about how he'd at first said the same words, the words about not knowing how to take care of a baby and gently squeezed Danceray's knee.

"You don't worry about takin care a Susan. Lige and Ivy and me got that covered. You just concentrate on lovin her. Babies can't have too much love or too much family."